For Dave,

Fragments

Thank You!

Catriona Mowat

CATRIONA MOWAT
AUTHOR

First published 2025 by Question Mark Horror

Fragments, Catriona Mowat

ISBN 978-1-0682179-1-3

Cover Design: Christy Aldridge, Grim Poppy Design

Edited by Heather Ann Larson, Indie Terror 13 Editing

Author Logo Design: Eddy Setiyawan

For Anthea, who loved a mystery more than anyone, and shared a love of the theatre, black lace parasols, and all things gothic.

I miss you, Mum.

Also by Catriona Mowat

-Beyond The Smoke And Shadow

A collection of nine gothic tales and poetry to haunt the darkest of nights. From the distant past to the far-off future, horrors lurk, and there are no happy endings. Pirates, witches, ghosts, cryptids, and death: what will you find waiting for you beyond the smoke and shadow?

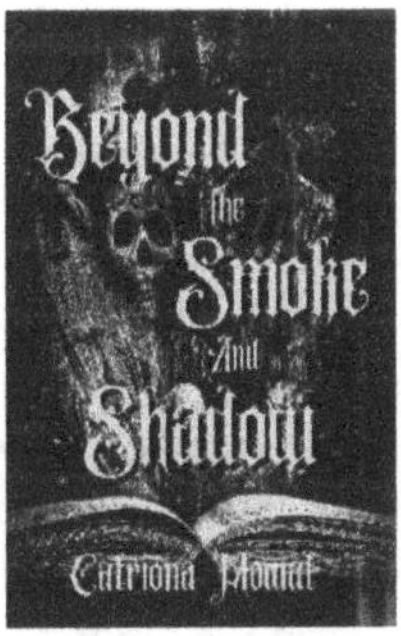

Available now on Amazon.
Signed copies available directly from the author
www.catrionamowat.sumupstore.com

Also available on the TikTok shop

Author's Note

Please be aware this novella has been written in UK English. When The UK and the US got divorced, you got the letter 'Z' and we got the letter 'U'. I don't know why, it was in the T&Cs, apparently.

Content warnings can be found at the back of the book to avoid spoilers.

Catriona
Mowat
Fragments

Fragments

Prologue

London, April 1774

The shadow was right behind her as she ran desperately looking for somewhere safe. All but the stagehands had left for the night, and they were nowhere to be found. She was alone with the darkness that sought her out.

Her hair was wild, her clothes bedraggled, and the bloom of a bruise was beginning to colour her cheek. She moved quickly through the rafters above the stage that was like home, throwing glances over her shoulder as she heard the dull sound of footsteps in the darkness behind her. Slow but steady, they were coming for her.

"Desdemona," a voice called to her.

The shadows seemed to move as she made her way across the narrow planks of wood that formed the bridge over the top of the stage, between an intricate pulley of ropes, lanterns, and fabrics, a system that she never quite understood.

Tears streaked her cheeks, twin rivers etched in the white paint on her face. Her deep-red lips, painted the colour of the richest wine, were smeared and bleeding, mixing blood and tears together in a grim communion.

She was almost across when the shadow pulled her back, a strong grip on her dress. The fabric began to tear, the rich red velvet slowly pulling apart fibre by fibre. Here eyes widened as she began to fall backwards.

"Please don't do this, I've done nothing! Help me, please!" the woman shouted into the darkness, but there were none there to hear other than the shadow that held her in a grip like iron.

Fingers wrapped around her small, pale throat, forcing her cries into silence as she began to choke. The pendant she wore around her neck was ripped away, falling to the stage below. Her eyes, once so clear and alive, turned red as her body fought for air.

"Spare your lies, you painted whore. Rot and perish, and be damned."

"Stop—" she tried to say through gasps for air that never came.

The hand that held her was joined by a rope, gently winding around her neck like the embrace of a lover.

Then she was falling.

Falling towards the stage, the wooden boards rising up to meet her, fiery glimmers from the gas lanterns throwing shadows across them. But the safety of solid ground eluded her. There was a jolt that sent pain through every fibre of her body, and she began to sway, suspended in the darkness, her lungs burning. Her eyes bled as the rope pulled taut around her throat, crushing the life from her body.

The shadow watched from above as she stilled, hanging halfway between heaven and earth.

"Goodbye, Desdemona. May you never know peace for your betrayal," the shadow whispered.

Only the creak of the rope in the darkness answered.

As the night deepened—shades of midnight-blue and black streaking the sky, creating shadows within shadows—the lonely workers tasked with damping the lanterns throughout the vast theatre arrived on the stage to complete their role.

The stage was empty.

The following evening, stage lights glowed and the cast assembled for their usual performance. But one of their number was missing. The leading lady, no less.

She would never be seen again.

Chapter 1

London, March 2025

Hazel looked up at the impressive façade of the Theatre Royal in Covent Garden. Her dyed grey hair shimmered silver in the light as the morning sun appeared from behind the dull cloud that was the usual uniform for the London sky. A white portico that bore the royal crest in vivid colours was supported by large columns bearing banners for the current Shakespearean season. Lanterns hung between the columns, the original remnants of the Victorian fittings. It looked from a distance like an ancient Greek temple, and she could feel that her journey was finally at its end. She was home.

She had been waiting for a position like this to open in the London theatre scene. It was her dream since she was a child to be involved with the West End. She finally combined her creative writing degree and her love of theatre—Playwright in Residence for a full season at the Theatre Royal, commissioned to craft a minimum of two original plays in the traditional theatre. The job title had a nice ring to it, and Hazel smiled to herself as she looked up at the theatre she would call her office for the next year. Her golden-tinted eyes sparkled with excitement.

She moved around the side of the building to the stage door, slightly hidden from view of the main entrance. It was sheltered by another wall of columns, painted a deep-blue colour. Otherwise, the grand white exterior of the building was forgotten here, the wall made of simple bricks.

A chill ran down her spine as she imagined all the actors, actresses, stage crew, and designers who had walked this path before her. While this was not the original theatre, destroyed in 1809 by a great fire that had torn the theatre district around Covent Garden apart, it was one of the oldest theatres in the city. And on this exact spot, a theatre had stood since the 1600s. Hazel could picture the throngs of people waiting to see their sweethearts of the stage, thousands of ghosts of cast, crew, and public all going before her.

As she reached the arched blue door set slightly inwards from the brick wall, the *Stage Door* sign slightly dulled where the gold paint had begun to peel and fade, Hazel took a deep breath.

"This is it," she said to herself, and pressed the buzzer.

"What is it? We're closed!" a stern voice replied through the small intercom next to the door.

"Oh, hello." She swallowed nervously. "My name is Hazel, Hazel Wilkins. I'm meant to be starting today as the new Playwright in Residence?" She had meant it to sound confident, but it came out as a question.

"The play-what?"

"The new writer. I'm supposed to meet Peter Warner for my induction?"

There was silence from the intercom.

Hazel was suddenly full of nerves. It would be so like her to get the day wrong. Ever since she was a kid, she had operated on a different level to everyone around her—creative, empathetic, and full of ideas and passion, but with absolutely no aptitude for schedules and rules. It had gotten her into trouble more than once in her life. Her mum had always said she had a touch of the spirits about her, that she was tuned in to a different realm.

Her parents died in a car accident when she was nineteen, and in the eight years since, she had often tried to see them in the vain hope that her mum had been right about her. Sometimes she caught a movement out of the corner of her eye in an empty room or smelled perfume that wasn't really there and felt a flurry of hope, but it never amounted to more than a faint glimmer. She had to dismiss it all as her imagination playing tricks on her to protect herself from disappointment. However much she wished that her parents were there to see her achieve her dreams, the ache of losing them again was too much.

The door in front of her suddenly opened, and a tall man who could only be described as 'portly' strode out, running a large hand through his slicked-back brown hair.

"Hazel? I'm Peter Warner, the theatre manager." He held out his hand for her to shake. He loomed over her, easily a foot taller than her. She was five foot two on a good day, he was surely over six feet. His green eyes had a kindness to them, and a redness in his cheeks and a neat beard gave him a gentleness that put her at ease straightaway.

She smiled warmly at him and shook his hand.

"Really nice to meet you, Mr Warner."

"Peter, please. Things move quickly enough here without us having to be formal. Now, we'll get you set up in an office shortly, but first, I'll give you a tour of the place. Keep to the places I tell you, and you'll get on just fine here, okay?" Hazel nodded.

Peter held the door open for her as she followed him into the depths of the backstage areas of the theatre. As she closed the door behind her, she caught the eye of the security guard stationed there, the intercom's microphone positioned on the desk beside him. He looked to be in his early seventies, with thinning white hair, a large bushy moustache, and dark eyes. The dour expression on his face unnerved her, until he suddenly winked, catching her off-guard.

"Welcome aboard, Hazel, Hazel Wilkins," he smirked.

"Thank you, Ralph. That will be all," said Peter in a stern voice, offering Hazel a small smile.

***

As Peter led her through the blank magnolia corridors towards the main foyer, Hazel lost her bearings. Each door along the corridors looked the same, each wall blending into another, until she found herself in the heart of a labyrinth. Suddenly, Peter opened a door and she found herself walking into the grand foyer. A large staircase loomed to her right, a wide sweeping stair that branched into two for access to the upper floors, overlooked by a great vaulted dome ceiling. A rich, red carpet covered the white marble stair, with large oil paintings of Shakesperean scenes adorning the pale-green walls. To the side of the staircase, a smaller circular staircase led down to the stalls beneath the main foyer, passing alcoves with grand statues.

"That's David Garrick on the left, and Arthur Lloyd on the right," Peter said, gesturing towards the statues. "Garrick owned the original theatre that stood here in the 1740s-1790s. Parts of the original theatre are still here in the foundations of the building, but it was mainly destroyed by a fire in the 1800s. Arthur Lloyd was a comedian and music hall man from the 1800s. The theatre is dedicated to him."

"The original theatre is still here? That's incredible," Hazel said, still taking in the grand surroundings.

"I knew you would be a theatre nerd like me. Yeah, down in the basement, but the area is out of bounds. We have some renovation work going on down there, so it's not safe." Hazel's face fell in disappointment as he spoke, and he patted her on the shoulder. "I'll get you some photos, how about that? Come on, time to see the actual theatre." He walked down the stairs and disappeared into the stalls.

As she descended the stairs behind him, she thought she saw a lady in a deep-red dress at the top of the stairs, watching her. But when she turned back to say hello, there was no one there.

Walking into the theatre itself, Hazel gasped. This was where her work would come to life. A gilded ceiling with three panels of vivid artwork displayed scenes from Hamlet, Swan Lake, and Aida—theatre, ballet, and opera all brought together under one roof. On either side of the large stage, the opera boxes with gilded borders and crests sat cloaked in darkness. The stage itself was a rich, deep wood.

Hazel climbed the small staircase to the side of the stage, by the orchestra pit, and stood on the creaking wood as Peter held up a finger and excused himself, his phone clamped to his ear. She could feel the very life of the theatre rooted in her feet on that stage. She exhaled slowly with a sigh of happiness, closing her eyes and taking in the feeling completely.

As she opened her eyes, she saw the woman from the lobby standing in one of the boxes by the stage, partially obscured by shadow. She was beautiful, with white hair and an opulent deep-red costume dress, and a cloak that draped around her shoulders with a graceful flare. She wore an expression of such sadness that Hazel's breath caught in her throat.

"Are you alright?" she said towards the shadowy box. The lights above the stage switched on with a sudden clunk, temporarily blinding her. Her hand up to shield her eyes, she tried to find the woman again, but she was gone.

Chapter 2

Hazel followed Peter through the backstage areas, meeting the rest of the crew, from set builders and lighting technicians to the box office admin team. She was pleasantly surprised to see Peter greet everyone in the team by name, which was not the case in many London theatres. He was clearly hands-on as a manager, and very popular, which was a good sign for her. He moved with an easy grace and a humble smile for everyone, and kindness radiated from him.

Finally, she was led to a small room at the far edge of the theatre that would be her office. It was sparsely furnished, with nothing but a desk with two chairs and a bookcase for her to use. But then, that was all she needed, and she was just grateful to be able to sit down after her long tour of the theatre. The backstage areas just seemed to go on forever, and she hadn't even made it up to the rafters yet.

Peter sat down with an exhausted sigh.

"So that's us, almost all of it. Was that too much for a day?" he asked.

"Maybe a little, but it's good to see everything," she replied. "I'll get lost a lot, though, I'm sure."

He laughed. "Don't worry, everyone does. Just keep a radio with you and someone will always come to your rescue."

After agreeing that they had done enough for one day, Hazel was dismissed for the evening.

Peter met her again at the stage door the next day, under the watchful eye of Ralph, and she was steered back to her office.

The two of them sat together for most of the day, going through Hazel's employment pack, paperwork, and the security information she would need. Finally, her new work ID was produced, and conversation turned to her upcoming projects.

"How are your ideas going? Will you have something special for us once we've finished our current production?" he asked expectantly, an awkward stillness filling the air.

"I have a few ideas just now. I'm sure I'll have something good," she lied. The truth was, she was feeling a bit overwhelmed, and her mind was utterly blank. But she reasoned that it was only her second day. The inspiration would come to her—it just had to. She could feel that there was something in this theatre, a story just waiting to be told if she would just listen.

***

In the basement, the team working on the renovations was busy replacing some of the old brickwork that lined the walls.

As Scott Collins removed bricks from a wall running around the outer edge of the basement, he suddenly gave a shout.

"Tom, get over here—I've found something!"

Tom Dennison, the team supervisor, stopped what he was doing and made his way across to Scott. He was fed up. The dimensions of the basement didn't match the measurements of the building by about two feet, and so far, everything that could go wrong had: crew sickness, lost tools, faulty equipment, all of it.

"What is it now?" he said, a tense annoyance in his voice. Scott looked up at him from his slightly crouched position, excitement shining in his golden eyes. In front of his face was a hole in the wall about level with Tom's chest, which Scott was shining a torch into. A cold draft poured out of the hole, chilling both men to the bone.

"You know how the blueprints didn't add up?" Scott said gleefully.

"Yeah …" Tom replied, his voice trailing off in confusion.

"That's because there's another wall behind this one! It's a storeroom or something, might be from the original theatre."

Tom reached out his hand to take the torch from Scott. "What are you talking about?"

Scott stood to his full height and stepped back to let Tom in. Bending slightly, Tom peered into the hole. The torchlight fell on a stone wall two feet further in, just like the measurements should have been. Dust covered the ground, untouched for the centuries that this wall had stood. A bundle of cloth lay on the floor, along with what looked to be a series of props. A sword and goblet glinted in the light, metal shining through the dust. And propped up against the outer wall, resting on top of a wooden trunk, was a painting. Unseen by human eyes for God knew how long, the gilded frame held the image of a beautiful woman, slightly turned to the side but still gazing at the viewer, her pale eyes looking out at an unseen audience, grey with flecks of a deep blue. Her nose was small and straight, her skin porcelain with rouged cheeks, which perfectly matched her white hair that curled over her shoulder in a perfect wave. Her full lips were a deep red, the colour of blood. Her hand was slightly raised, holding on to a large gold-and-ruby pendant in the shape of a star around her neck.

Tom gasped.

"Go and get Warner. He needs to see this."

A shadow flashed across the beam of the torch, as if heading out of the hidden room and into the world.

***

Peter had just gotten to his feet ready to leave Hazel's office when the radio clipped to his belt suddenly burst to life.

"Peter, this is Scott on the reno team. We need you down here urgently."

"Copy that, on my way," Peter replied, holding the radio to his mouth. He looked at Hazel, an uneasy smile on his face. "Duty calls. Good luck with your masterpiece. Call if you need anything." With that, he left the room.

Alone for the first time since entering the theatre, Hazel exhaled deeply and sat back in her chair. The woman she had seen in the theatre box crossed her mind. The sad expression on the woman's face had been haunting. Hazel knew she needed to find and help her somehow.

It's none of my business, she thought to herself. *Leave the actresses alone.*

But what if there is a story there? Melancholy like that doesn't come from nothing, the devil on her shoulder answered the angel. The angel was silent, and so Hazel decided. She would find the lady.

***

That afternoon it was the talk of the entire backstage crew. A secret store had been found in the bowels of the theatre. By five p.m., the entire theatre team was gathered in the main foyer just in time to see the painting being brought up from the basement. There was a collective gasp when it emerged into the foyer—the rich colours were so vivid, the image so life-like that you could almost see the lady breathing on the canvas. The painting was hung in a space on the wall at the top of the main staircase, the subject calmly surveying every visitor to the theatre.

When the atmosphere had calmed and most of the team returned to their tasks, Hazel stood in front of the painting. She was almost caught in a daze, unable to look away and almost sure that the pale lady was staring back at her. She knew it; this was the same sad and beautiful lady she had seen in the theatre box.

But that can't be right, she thought. *Was Mum right about me all along?*

A small plaque sat at the base of image, firmly set into the frame. It read *C.R. as Desdemona; London 1774.*

A whisper sounded in her ear, a disembodied woman's voice that seemed to whirl and disappear like dust in a sunbeam.

"Remember me."

The world spun, and she felt herself falling forwards, her vision swirling in hues of gold, ruby, and white as the painting rose up to meet her.

Fragments

Chapter 3

London, November 1773

Charlotte Robinson waited at the edge of the stage as the play came to an end. Horatio cradled Hamlet's body as the dead lay scattered across the stage. No matter how many times she watched from the wings, Charlotte fought the urge to run onto the stage and tell Hamlet everything would be alright and wipe the tears from Horatio's cheeks. Every night. A tear of her own slid down her cheek, and she quickly patted it dry, afraid of smearing her porcelain-white makeup.

As the play came to its end, Fortinbras firmly seated on the gilded wooden throne, the applause began. It rolled through the very floor of the stage like a great peal of thunder that the actors could feel in their chests.

Charlotte walked on stage to be greeted by an even greater wave of claps, cheers, and roses thrown at her feet. Genuine tears of gratitude pricked her eyes. She was the darling of the London theatre society, and with each performance, they became more enamoured with her.

Her Ophelia had been the talk of the town for three months now, her beauty the subject of works of art and songs. Each night, a crowd of admirers waited for her, just to catch a glimpse as she left the theatre. Invitations to every ball and salon in the city lined her dressing room.

At twenty-three, Charlotte was a stunning beauty. Hair so light it was almost white, it curled in a natural wave that seemed to sit perfectly as if commanded by the angels themselves to rest gracefully on her slim shoulders. Her matching pale skin, made even whiter by the stage paint, made her look like a porcelain doll, fragile and delicate. Her full lips and natural pout invited those around to gather closely for a kiss, although her demure nature would of course forbid it. Small in stature, her waif-like body only enhanced the beauty of her expressive face, with a nose that would crinkle with both amusement and derision and large eyes that could pierce a man's soul. Despite her fragile appearance, which could easily mistake her as a damsel in distress, Charlotte commanded every room she entered. The stage was her home, each audience held enraptured by her every word.

Soaking in the praise for a moment before Mr Garrick stepped forwards for his moment as Claudius, Charlotte sighed happily. This was their final performance of the tragedy, and soon rehearsals would begin for a new production of *Othello*.

Charlotte was sad to leave Ophelia behind; she had grown to love the tragic madness of Ophelia's loss and her almost-freeing way of drifting through each scene. She was part of the world but isolated in her ethereal haze of flowers and grief, and Charlotte felt a kinship in her soul with the character.

As she removed her makeup and costume for the final time, she heard a knock at the dressing room door.

"Come in!" she called, adjusting her dress in a hurry.

The door opened, and Mr Garrick walked in. Despite his short stature, Garrick was a force of nature, with an aquiline nose and deep-brown eyes that somehow made him warm and empathetic as a heroic actor and cold and calculating when playing the villain. He was no stranger to food and wine, with a ruddy complexion that stood out even more against his powdered, white wig and a rotund figure to show for it.

"Good evening, Charlotte. You were radiant tonight, as ever. Your Ophelia has captured many a heart, I'd wager," Garrick said with a wink.

"Thank you, Mr Garrick. Your Claudius was certainly impressive. I truly felt your words in my soul."

Before he could reply, a tall man appeared in the doorway behind Garrick. He had a stern face with a hooked nose, small eyes that looked almost black, and thin lips that seemed to naturally scowl. He gazed at Charlotte as he stepped out from the shadow of the corridor.

Garrick jumped, suddenly aware of his presence.

"Charlotte, this is…Fred. Fred York. He is a close friend of mine and an admirer of yours. I promised him an introduction."

Fred York stepped forwards and took Charlotte's hand, kissing it. "I am a most ardent admirer, and I am delighted to meet you at last."

Charlotte smiled a smile that didn't quite reach her eyes. There was something about this man that she found unnerving, something in his manner. Still, she smiled politely. She was used to men waiting at the stage door for her, but for Garrick to personally escort this man to her, he must be of some importance. She could tell from the nervous, intense look from Garrick that she needed to give a second performance that evening—the act of charm and grace in the face of evil.

"I am most delighted to meet you, Mister York. I trust my performance was to your liking?" she said, her voice thick with false sweetness.

His black eyes gazed at her, unblinking. He still held her hand in his, his thumb gently pressing on her fingers.

"You were simply perfect yet again, as I anticipated. I hear that you are to take up the mantle of Desdemona in the upcoming season. Your delicate features and sweet nature lend themselves perfectly to the part." His compliment paid, he nodded to Garrick.

Garrick stepped forwards.

"Yes, Charlotte will be the Desdemona that all others look to, of that we can be sure." He coughed, a nervousness filling his limbs as he hopped subtly from one leg to the other.

"Charlotte, I have arranged a dinner for the two of you for tomorrow evening. Here, in the theatre."

Charlotte's blood ran cold at the thought of being alone with York, but she could tell from Garrick's face that it was not a request. It was a command.

She nodded slowly.

"Until tomorrow, my dear," Mr York said, kissing her hand again and finally releasing it.

She flexed her fingers, feeling the freedom within them. A shiver ran down her spine as the door closed behind the departed gentlemen. Dinner tomorrow. She would have to break that news to James.

James and Charlotte were childhood sweethearts, forever bonded together with a deep companionship and a quiet passion that burned within them both. James had grown into a handsome man with chiselled features, deep-blue eyes the colour of sapphires, and sandy-blond hair. Charlotte and James had been secretly married four years prior in a quiet ceremony with only their parents present to witness the event, and lived honestly within their means.

James was a quiet, measured man. He was employed as a parish clerk, known for being kind and responsible with all who encountered him. His sweetness matched that of Charlotte, and together they were two halves of one whole. They had agreed that Charlotte's star would burn brighter if she was seen to be unattached. It wounded them both, but they had been proven correct. Charlotte was careful to avoid any situations that could lead to complications, and for the last few years, that had worked wonderfully. She was seen to be the perfect woman, available yet wholly unattainable.

But there was something about this Mr York that Charlotte suspected wouldn't accept that easily. She wished now more than ever that James could step into the light beside her. But she knew it was too late. Garrick would not let that happen now.

Alone in her dressing room, Charlotte sank into the chair by the mirror, gazing at her reflection. Her eyes brimmed with tears. She was tired of the pretence, the public claim on her time and affection, and the way that someone like Fred York could barge his way into her private life. Forever surrounded by people, Charlotte had never felt more alone.

Chapter 4

London, March 2025

Hazel gasped as the world came rushing back to her, her feet firmly planted back in the lobby of the Theatre Royal with the painting in front of her. She had seen inside a fragment of memory, but it belonged to someone else. Charlotte Robinson. The name settled on her as if she had always known it, as if she felt the lady in the painting in her very bones. And as surely as she knew Charlotte's name, she knew something terrible had happened to her.

The afternoon light was dimming through the foyer windows as she made her way towards the staff corridors, which were eerily empty. Glancing at her watch, she could see she had been trapped in the fragment of the past for an hour, and the majority of staff had gone for their break before the evening show began. Tonight was the final performance of *Much Ado About Nothing*, and tomorrow, the run of *Hamlet* would begin, to finish the theatre's *Season of Shakespeare*.

As she made her way through the quiet corridors towards her office, unsure if she was headed the right way, Peter appeared around a corner just ahead of her. His gaze was fixed on his watch as he came into view.

"Peter!"

He jumped, startled at the sound. Looking up, he took in Hazel and exhaled deeply.

"Oh, Hazel! You made me jump. How are you?"

"Honestly? I'm not sure. I am a little—out of sorts, I guess. I'm sorry, you must be in a hurry. But may I ask you a question?"

"Of course. What can I help with?" He glanced at his watch again.

"Where can I find records of the history of the theatre? Information about performances, actors, things like that? Going back to the Garrick years?"

"The Garrick years? Well, that is quite a way back, my dear. A lot of those records could well have been destroyed by the fire. You can try the online archive; most surviving records will have been scanned in there. Otherwise, you'll have to go to the archives in person. What is it you're looking for?"

"I'm not sure exactly, but I think I'm looking for information on an actress from the Garrick years. I think she's the woman in the painting they found downstairs."

"Really? How fascinating. What makes you think that?" he said, not entirely paying attention to the conversation.

"Just a hunch, I guess. Well, thank you, Peter. How can I access the online archive?"

"I'll send you a link." Peter took his mobile phone out of his pocket and typed a few words. "There you are, done. Now, if you'll excuse me, I must be getting on. Good luck with your research, Hazel." With that, he left.

"Thank you!" Hazel called after him as he disappeared around the next corner.

As she made her way down corridor after corridor, she realised she was lost. She slumped against the wall, reaching for the radio at her side. Her hand grasped nothing. A picture came to mind—her radio sitting neatly on her desk beside her laptop, right where she left it.

"Great. Just great, Hazel. Can't even find your own office, and you forget your radio. Brava," she said to herself.

There was a sound like rustling leaves that caught her attention, coming from behind a door in front of her. *Someone's here, they can help me get back*, Hazel thought as she turned the handle to the dressing room ahead of her.

As she stepped inside, leaving the door slightly open behind her, she couldn't help but feel a sense of familiarity, as if she had been in this room—or a room very like it—before even though she knew she hadn't. The room was small, with dark wooden panelling on the bottom half of the wall and a cream-coloured wallpaper above. The walls were lined with posters and playbills from past performances. The furniture was relatively sparse, with a costume rack laden with velvet and lace on one side of the room. An open door on the far wall led to a small ensuite bathroom, and on the right-hand side of the room was a vanity desk with a lighted mirror for stage makeup. It was littered with paint, powder, eyeliners, lipsticks, and mascaras, as well as hair-pins and curlers. The only thing that was missing? The person whose room it was.

The rustling sound came again, this time from the bathroom, ahead of her. The air felt heavy.

"Hello?" she called out. "Sorry to barge in. Can you help me get to the writing department?"

There was no reply.

Hazel knocked on the open bathroom door as she peered inside. "Hello?"

The bathroom was empty.

As she turned back, she caught a glimpse of movement in the mirror, a flash of deep red darting in front of the costume rack. It was following by a loud cracking sound just as she turned her head away from the mirror.

A circular crack appeared in the centre of the mirror, creating a web of fractures that snaked out to the edges of the frame. Small chips of glass lay scattered amongst the beauty supplies on the table in a beautiful but dangerous tableau.

She approached the glass, a fragmented reflection looking back at her, contorted and multiplied. In a large shard, a face appeared over her shoulder, pale skin, white hair, and a dark, painted mouth open in a scream that pierced the quiet. As the sound thundered in her mind, a wave of sadness overcame Hazel.

It was her.

Hazel's breath caught in her throat. She blinked, squeezing her eyes shut for half a second longer than usual to block out the grief and fear overwhelming her senses. When she opened them, there was no one there.

Gone in the blink of an eye, the door slammed shut, leaving her alone in the silent room.

She darted into the corridor, but there was no sign of the pale woman in red. Instead, she came face to face with an athletic woman with red hair, thin, angular features, and green eyes. She recognised her from a photo on the playbill—Marianne, whose room she had just run out of.

"Can I help you? What were you doing in my dressing room?" Marianne said, suspicion in every note of her voice.

"Oh, I'm sorry, I was looking for someone for directions. I'm Hazel, the new playwright. I'm really sorry, but something happened to your mirror, I can't explain."

Marianne looked confused. There was a slight pause as she registered what Hazel said before she rushed to the doorway of her room.

"What do you mean? It looks fine to me."

Hazel peered into the room over Marianne's shoulder. Marianne was right—the mirror was pristine.

"I—I—I'm sorry, I must have been wrong. I thought I saw a crack in it. I'm so sorry." Hazel turned to leave, panic rising in her chest.

"Wait, hold on there. Are you alright? Come inside, you're shaking." Marianne put an arm around Hazel and ushered her into the room.

Sitting her at the makeup table, Marianne headed into the bathroom, returning with a glass of water. She placed it in front of Hazel. She exuded warmth, a comfort Hazel wasn't used to, and she couldn't help but think she might be able to call this woman a friend.

Marianne's eyes swam with concern.

"You look white as a sheet! What's wrong?"

"Honestly?" Hazel said, sipping the water, speaking without a moment of hesitation. "I don't know. I swear I'm losing my mind. I'm seeing things that aren't there. Do you believe in ghosts?"

Marianne smirked a little, her thin mouth made even thinner with the half-smile.

"Like wearing a sheet, floating through walls ghosts?"

"I guess so." Hazel felt herself relax as she smiled a little. "Maybe without the sheet and with actual clothes on, though."

"Well, I can't say I do. Seeing is believing, I suppose. You look like shit, though, so I believe you think you saw something." Marianne put a hand on Hazel's shoulder.

The simple, calm gesture sent a wave of warmth shooting down her arms and into her fingers. She flexed them, letting her fingers dance in the light of the mirror, entranced.

"Hazel? Are you okay?" Marianne's voice drew Hazel out of her reverie.

"Hmm? Oh, yeah. I'll be okay. Thank you for everything." She stood. "Sorry, I'm keeping you from getting ready for the show tonight."

"Yeah, I probably should get cracking. *Much Ado* might not work as well without Beatrice, she's pretty key to the plot. But come and see me again sometime. I'm usually here, and it's nice to have a friend outside of the cast."

After making a promise to come back, Marianne gave Hazel the directions she needed to find her way back and they said their goodbyes.

***

Back in her office, Hazel powered on her laptop and opened her emails. The link from Peter was still sitting at the top of her inbox, and she quickly found her way into the archive with a registered account.

SEARCH TERM "Charlotte+Robinson"

Filtering through the results for modern actresses and stage news featuring the same name, Hazel eventually came across what she was looking for—a playbill for *Hamlet*, performed in 1773. The cast on the poster featured David Garrick as King Claudius and one Charlotte Robinson as Ophelia. It all fit with what she had seen.

A series of newspaper articles from *The London Chronicle* in 1774 also appeared on the search results, and Hazel felt a chill in the air as she clicked on it, her breath misting in front of her as the temperature dropped significantly.

3rd April 1774 Evening Edition

GARRICK'S DARLING MIDNIGHT FLIT

Charlotte Robinson, darling of society and star of the stage, has disappeared in the night.

Her lauded performances at the Theatre Royal, Drury Lane, have long been praised as highly as her beauty. The darling of David Garrick, Miss Robinson has delighted audiences of rich and poor alike yet again these past three months with her performances as Desdemona in Garrick's season of Othello.

The circumstances of Miss Robinson's disappearance are a mystery. James Robinson, the actress's little-seen husband, cannot be found for comment but is not believed to be with her. Rumours abound that Miss Robinson may have eloped with a lover or may be the victim of a crime.

***

2nd May 1774, Morning Edition

STAGE DIVA STILL MISSING

Miss Robinson, stage star and society jewel, remains missing, with fears for her life now on the tips of the tongues of all society. Some report a sinister plot on the life of the ingénue, with sightings of the actress accompanied by a distinguished yet menacing gentleman in the months leading up to her disappearance. The gentleman's identity has not been divulged, but is confirmed not to be her husband, James Robinson, whom the world learned of only a matter of days before her disappearance. He too has not been sighted for some weeks.

David Garrick has not commented on the loss of the stage beauty, yet the well-regarded actor and theatre owner has been seen shedding a tear when asked about Miss Robinson. Does Garrick know more than he utters?

Patronage of the theatre has recently been given by none other than the Prince of Wales and Duke of York, but with a scandal of this scale emerging, Garrick's position in the theatre, and in society, may be endangered.

Hazel closed the article with a sigh, shivering from the chill in the room. *Disappeared without a trace? What happened to you, Charlotte?*

The cold in the room seemed to wrap around her, swirling and settling on her skin and in her bones.

"Charlotte? Are you here?"

A whisper in her ear seemed to come from everywhere and nowhere all at once.

"I have always been here."

"What do you want from me?" Hazel asked, shivering not just from the cold.

"Help me. Find me."

The cold that enveloped Hazel shifted and moved, letting the warmth of the room filter back again. Hazel caught a glimpse of a hazy figure with white hair and red lips appearing at the door, staring at her.

Charlotte held Hazel's gaze for a moment then disappeared through the door.

Rushing to the door, Hazel opened it and rushed into the corridor—

Fragments

Chapter 5

London, December 1773

The hallway was dimly lit with candles mounted on the wall. In many circumstances, the warm glow would be calming, almost romantic. But Charlotte felt fear rising in her as she made her way to the private room Garrick had commanded her to. She knew what waited for her there. Mister York.

For the last month, he had been a constant presence at the end of rehearsals for the new run, a shadow that infested her life with darkness and wouldn't let go.

Private dinners by candlelight, roses, jewellery—Mister York spared no expense in his bombardment of affection for her. She was overwhelmed, her position in society as both an actress and a woman such that she could be traded and sold by the men around her like chattel. The only man who did not attempt to own her? Her sweet James, the only man to actually own a piece of her heart and soul.

But not even James had been able to help her escape the admirations of Mister York. Garrick merely ensured that he was kept away from the theatre.

It would be inappropriate, my dear. Your adoring crowds would not be amused by his presence. You are the belle of society, and you must keep it that way if we are to survive. The theatre is in financial danger, and if we are to carry on, we need patronage, Garrick's voice echoed in her mind.

Standing in front of the door to Garrick's private suite at the back of the theatre, Charlotte paused, a deep sigh building as she contemplated her future. She was a prisoner in her own life, and she could feel the bars of social pressure and powerlessness as surely as if they were iron.

As she raised her hand to the door handle, it swung open, and Mister York stood before her.

"Charlotte, my dear, here you are. I thought I heard your delicate footsteps some moments ago. Are you alright?"

"Good evening, Mister York," she mumbled, a small smile that didn't reach her eyes flashing on her face. "My apologies, I was merely caught in a dream. Shall we dine?" She motioned behind him to the table beyond, candles lit and a covered silver platter of food waiting for them.

"Quite right, we shall. Please, join me." He held out a hand to her, which she accepted, a small shiver of revulsion moving down her body.

"Your rehearsals move apace. How long before the public are permitted the joy of your presence on stage?" he asked once they were seated, unveiling a large game pie on the silver platter.

She shifted uncomfortably in her chair under his gaze. Polite, yes, but there was an unspoken threat that radiated from him. She had no reason to think his intentions were anything but honourable, but her gut told her to run whenever he looked at her.

"We shall be performing in the new year. Mister Garrick believes we still have much work to do, but we shall be ready. It is a most complex performance."

"Complex, maybe, but you shall rise to the occasion, of that I am confident. Although, I do worry that Garrick pushes you too hard."

"Thank you, sir. I am sure he only wishes the best for the play, and for the theatre. I encourage direction when it is warranted."

"Well, fret not. I shall be there each day to ensure that you are not worked too hard," he said as he sliced the pie with a large knife and handed her a plate.

"And I shall ensure that you are not troubled by any man." The unspoken threat was clear.

Her mind shifted to James, a panic filling her heart. If he were to be seen with her now, he would be in danger. She couldn't allow anything to happen to him.

"I assure you, Mister York, I am in no need of a bodyguard. You need not attend daily rehearsals. Surely it will spoil your appetite for the first performance?"

"On the contrary, my dear. Witnessing your triumphant rise to glory step by step shall bring me great joy. And I shall be your companion for gala events and evening journeys."

Charlotte grimaced, although this went unnoticed by York.

"Your faithful shadow, always." His black eyes flashed.

"Mister York, it strikes me that you offer so much of your time to me, yet I know nothing about you. Where were you born? What do you do? You must have other responsibilities?"

"Nothing to note, and where I have been is of no import. These are trifling matters when compared with your beauty and grace." His tone was firm. Charlotte knew she would learn nothing of this dark and sinister creature tonight.

Shrinking back in her seat, she took a small bite of the pie, all the while watched by Fred York.

***

An hour later, Charlotte sat in her dressing room, removing the carefully-applied paint that highlighted her porcelain skin, crystal eyes, and full lips. It had become her signature, a sure way of people recognising and remembering her. Over time, it had become her mask, her armour, hiding her true face and soul from the world.

A knock at the door startled her from her task.

"Hello?" she called.

David Garrick stepped into the room.

"How was dinner, my dear?"

She sighed. "It was the same as ever, Mr Garrick. We talked of nothing but the play and myself. I know nothing about him, but something makes me uneasy. Why do you insist on my entertaining him?"

"I cannot say why, only that it is important for all of our futures. Please, Charlotte, you must understand that."

"But what of James? You know this breaks my heart to not have him near the theatre at all. We agreed to keep our marriage a secret from all but you, but I didn't agree to be a whore for your friends."

A resounding slap broke the tension in the room. Garrick lowered his hand, flexing his fingers, as she placed a hand on her reddening cheek, tears welling in her eyes. Her face throbbed.

"That is enough, Charlotte!" he shouted. His voice quickly calmed as he looked at her weeping form. He sighed.

"I am sorry for striking you, girl, but your selfish dreams of love must end here. You and James know why he must not be known; nothing has changed. I ask you not to whore around, but to entice York to our goodwill." He sighed as she dried her eyes.

"But whatever your feelings for Fred, you have done well. He sent me to deliver this, with his fond regards." He handed her a piece of cloth rolled into a neat form.

As she took it from him, she was surprised at how much weight was contained in that small roll.

Placing the parcel on the table in front of her, she unrolled the cloth. There was a flash of gold and red, and then it was before her—a heavy gold chain, ending with a gold and ruby pendant. As she picked it up, she could see that the pendant consisted of an ornate square of gold with swirling patterns and engraved lines sitting atop a rounded base. In the centre and in each corner of the gilt square sat a round ruby with smaller stones set within the embellishment. The overall appearance was that of a star. This was the kind of jewellery that would have befit royalty.

"It is exquisite," she breathed. "I can't possibly accept this."

"You can, and you will. He also asked me to give you this note." He handed her a heavy parchment.

Reading the swirls of ink on the page, her stomach felt like it was filled with lead.

My dear Charlotte,

This pendant may not hold a candle to your beauty, but it would please me to know that you wear it close to your heart each day.

As Othello himself would say, I love thee. And when I love thee not, chaos is come again.

You are mine as I am yours.

-F

Charlotte folded the parchment and handed it back to Garrick.

"This cannot endure. It will end badly; you know it will." Tears once again pricked at the edges of her eyes.

"Charlotte, I will not hear it. His intentions are for your good. Why can you not see that?"

"I am afraid of him, afraid of what he might do."

"Nonsense, Charlotte. This is not a fantasy; you are not playing a damsel in need of rescue. This is life, and York is well placed to secure our future in society. You have no idea how powerful he really is. He is a gentleman and will not see you come to harm."

"And what of James?"

"What of him? Love him, and love him well, but not in the eyes of others. He may ruin everything. It is up to you to secure our patronage."

"Why must all of our futures rest on me? Please don't make me do this!" she pleaded, reaching out to Garrick. He shook her off.

"You are the one he has chosen for his attention. This is what must be. The sooner you accept that, the easier it will be. Now please, get some rest and forget your fears." With that, he left the room, letting the door forcefully shut behind him.

Alone in her room, Charlotte gazed at the pendant and letter, Garrick's words echoing in her mind alongside the final words from York.

You have no idea how powerful he really is.

You are mine as I am yours.

Locking eyes with her reflection, she placed the pendant around her neck and stared at herself. Caught in a current she couldn't escape, she felt herself being washed away, dragged into oblivion by powerful men who owned her, however much she resisted.

Picking up a brass snuff box that lay on the table, she threw it, shattering the mirror. Watching the fragments of glass explode towards her, small cuts on her porcelain skin appearing as the glass lay glittering in the light on the table, she screamed.

It was a scream of isolation, of fear, and of loss.

The world dissolved.

Chapter 6

London, March 2025

With a gasp, Hazel found herself back in the empty corridor outside her office.

"Charlotte, where are you? What happened to you?" she whispered to the empty hallway.

"Remember me," came a disembodied whisper in response.

***

The following day, she sat at her laptop and began to write. Everything she had seen of Charlotte, everything she had heard. Before she knew it, she had formed part of a script.

This is how I help her, she realised. *Remember her by writing a play about her disappearance.*

Opening the browser, she went back to the archive. Garrick had mentioned needing patronage for the theatre, but she was sure she had seen that the Royal Family had given their patronage to the theatre. She quickly found the articles again and confirmed her suspicion.

"Who are you, Fred York?"

A quick search for a Fred York in 1770's London yielded results that chilled her to her core.

His Royal Highness, Frederick, Duke of York and Albany. Second son of the King & Queen of Britain.

Looking at images, she felt the world shift beneath her. It was him, the man she had seen in the fragments of Charlotte's memory.

You have no idea how powerful he really is.

She felt the chill in the air return as she thought of Garrick's words to Charlotte. It had been a warning of something else entirely, she realised.

Searching for information on the Duke of York, Hazel discovered he left London in late 1774 to help the British Army quell rebellion in the New World colonies. The Americans eventually sent the British army running back with their tails between their legs, and the duke returned to London by 1780 after failed attempts to reclaim the country from their Declaration of Independence. He returned to military action in France in the 1790s.

"Sentenced to a life overseas, are you hiding something, Your Highness?" she said to the empty room. There was no reply.

***

Falling into a focus she had not felt before, Hazel embellished her script, adding her own flourishes to Charlotte's life. Her time in Charlotte's memories made her feel as if she knew her better than anyone, and she could easily recount her life.

The radio sputtering to life brought her out of her task as the thin, reedy voice of the aging security guard came through.

"Hazel, Hazel Wilkins, are you still in the building?" She looked at the time: 11:30 p.m. She had lost track of time completely.

"Aw, shit!" she said to herself before pressing the radio.

"Hi, Ralph. Yeah, I'm still here. Sorry, I lost track of time. I'll finish up soon and get going."

"No skin off my nose, do what you want. I'll lock up around you."

"Would it be ok for me to see the stage before I go? I need to get an idea of the space."

There was a pause on the other end of the radio, then a sigh. "Fine. Let me know when you're done so I can lock up. Some of us have got a job to do, you know."

"You are a star, thank you."

"Hmm."

Hazel suppressed a smile. Ralph was a curmudgeon, but she could tell he was a good man with a wicked sense of humour, and she respected that.

Finishing her scene then locking her office behind her, she made her way to the stage. For the first time, she managed to find her way there without issue, and this sent a jolt of pride through her. She was part of the theatre now.

The auditorium was empty, emergency lighting sending a sinister green glow over the stalls as she looked out over them. The stage was dark, her footsteps creaking on the wood in the echoing silence around her. Using her phone to light her way, she walked across to the other side of the stage, trying to get a sense of the space for her stage directions. She stood for a moment, taking in her environment, when she heard a noise.

Drip.

Drip.

Drip.

The noise was regular, rhythmic. It was accompanied by a low creaking sound she couldn't place. She turned, squinting into the darkness beyond the small circle of light offered by her phone.

The noise seemed to be right beside her, but there was nothing there.

She looked up, and screamed.

A woman was swinging, her slack and lifeless body hanging in the air above the stage, a red dress visible above a pair of silken shoes. Blood was dripping from those shoes, the rope above her creaking as it moved in the dark. White hair and pale skin made paler still in death, a grotesque tableau of the grave. Charlotte.

Falling to the stage floor, Hazel scrabbled backwards, desperate to get away from the grisly scene above. Nausea roiled in her stomach as she squeezed her eyes shut against the vision.

"What in hell's bells is going on in here?" a voice carried from the auditorium.

Hazel's eyes snapped open. The grisly scene was gone. Ralph made his way down the aisle of stall seats, his torch fixed on Hazel.

"I heard a scream when I was locking the foyer. What in the bloody hell are you doing?"

As he reached the foot of the stage, his face relaxed with sympathy. He could see the fear etched on her face, the tears still wet on her cheeks, her mouth slack as she drew in ragged breaths. He climbed the steps to the stage and put a hand on her shoulder.

"Hazel? Are you alright? What happened to you?"

She looked at him as the world came back into focus. "Did you see her?" Her voice was croaky, barely louder than a whisper.

"See who? There's no one here 'cept you and me." He patted her shoulder.

"Charlotte. She was here. Hanging. Bloody. You must have seen her; she was right here!"

"I think you need to get home and get some rest. There's no one here."

"The blood!" She darted forward, dragging herself to her feet. "There is blood on the stage, look!" She pointed to a dark stain on the wood where a clear puddle of blood had formed under Charlotte's feet.

Ralph squinted.

"There's nothing there. What are you talking about?" He moved his foot over the stage where she pointed, emphasising the point.

He sighed. "Hazel, go home. You need to take a day out or something, get yourself sorted out. Maybe you should get yourself to the doctors. They have pills for everything nowadays."

He led her through the maze of backstage corridors, mumbling about psychiatric wards and complaining about having to babysit.

Hazel heard nothing, lost in her thoughts of Charlotte.

Murder or suicide? Where did you go?

They reached the stage door, and Ralph gave her a pitying look as he opened it for her. "Get yourself some help."

"Thank you, Ralph. I'm sorry."

He nodded with a grunt and closed the door behind her.

***

That night, Hazel's waking dreams were filled with necklaces of gold and of rope. She saw Charlotte swinging in the dark, blood falling as she choked and strained for salvation. She saw dark eyes knitted together in fury as a figure in shadows looked down from above Charlotte's swaying body.

Unable to escape from the vision of what she witnessed earlier that evening, and accepting that sleep was not going to come easily, she sat in a chair by her bedroom window, a small room in a London flat that she shared with three others she had known since university. Time and life had stepped in, and now they all kept to themselves despite the fact they had been friends for years. Her bedroom was her haven, and she needed that now more than ever.

Picking up a notebook and pen, she wrote furiously. Scene notes, dialogue, stage directions—the entire play was plotted, discarded, and re-plotted. Each variation of her notes touched on the spirit of the woman Hazel had come to know and love from her snatches of memory, but she failed to capture her loneliness and despair. By the time morning dawned, the pale early rays gently touching her skin, crumpled paper lay heaped around her.

It's no use. I need to be at the theatre, she thought to herself. A quick shower and a swipe of makeup later, she was on her way back.

She arrived at the theatre at the same time as Peter. One look at his face when he saw her approach was enough to tell her Ralph had left him a message about the events of the evening.

"Hazel, I wasn't expecting you in today. Are you alright? Ralph said you took a funny turn last night."

"I'm fine, I'm fine." She waved his questions off. "I had a bit of a bad night, but I'm alright, and I need to work on the play. It won't write itself."

"Are you sure? Ralph said some strange things."

"I'm sure. I promise, I'm fine. If you don't mind, I'll get to it." She strode away before he had a chance to object.

Before she headed to her office, she needed to go back to the stage. She knew she wasn't seeing things; it had really happened. Striding with a purpose, she navigated the backstage corridors with an ease she hadn't noticed before.

Just as she was almost past the dressing rooms, she bumped into Marianne.

"Oh, Hazel, hi! We have to stop bumping into each other like this. One of us will get bruised." She frowned as she properly looked at Hazel. She had dark circles under her eyes barely hidden by makeup, a dull, glassy look in her eyes, and sunken cheeks. This didn't look like the Hazel that Marianne had met the day before yesterday.

"Are you alright? No offence, but you look like shit."

Hazel laughed at Marianne's bluntness. "I didn't sleep well. I guess I'm just tired. Sorry, I didn't mean to bump into you."

"You sure you're just tired? You haven't been seeing things again, have you?"

Hazel sighed. Marianne had already seen her lose it; she may as well tell her the truth.

"Honestly, yes. Last night, I saw something awful. I know it sounds wild, but I'm not imagining things. Come with me, I'll show you."

Taking Marianne by the hand, Hazel took her to the stage.

"Here. She was hanged here, I saw it. There was blood on the stage, but Ralph couldn't see it." Hazel stopped short, her gaze fixed on something in the auditorium.

Charlotte was back, standing in one of the boxes, watching her.

"She's right there. Can you see her?" she asked, pointing at Charlotte.

"Hazel, I'm worried about you. See who? Who was hanged? What blood?"

Hazel let out a growl of frustration.

"No one else can see her, but she's right there! Come with me."

She led Marianne down the steps and through the auditorium to the foyer, coming to a stop in front of the portrait of Charlotte.

"This is her, Charlotte Robinson. She's haunting me. It sounds nuts, I know it does, but she's here in the theatre. She went missing, but I know she was murdered on that stage. I have to tell her story. I just have to."

"Hazel, take it easy. You're rambling." Marianne rested a hand on Hazel's cheek. She moved to the portrait and took a closer look at the plaque.

"C.R. How do you know her name was Charlotte—Robinson, was it?"

"I found her in the archives. She was an actress in the 1770s here in the original theatre. Plus, I've been seeing things, fragments of her life. It's like going back in time."

"Okay, slow down. So, the woman in this painting is a ghost that's haunting you, and you've been dreaming about her life?"

"Yes, you understand!" Hazel said with relief flooding her voice.

"I understand. Hazel, I think you might need to speak to Peter about taking some time off. You're clearly under a lot of pressure, and this portrait thing is getting to you. You're shaking like a leaf, and you haven't slept. Get some help."

"I'm sick of telling people I'm fine. I am. I just need to help her. You might not believe me, but she's here."

"Tell you what. I have a friend; she works in a crystal and tarot shop—witchcraft supplies. Her boss does readings. They might be able to help. Why don't I call them for you?"

"Why would you help me?"

"Because I like you, Hazel. And I'm not going to stand here and watch you drive yourself nuts over a painting, however mysterious it might be." She looked at Hazel and sighed, her eyes wide with pity. The silence between them echoed.

"Come on, let's go call Chloe. You're staying with me for a few days, no objections."

As the two women left the lobby in the direction of Marianne's dressing room, Charlotte watched them go, sad, grey-blue eyes chasing their departure, a sense of hope and longing in the air. A sound caught her attention for a moment, the dull sound of footsteps echoing from the empty staircase.

She turned.

A disembodied shadow headed directly for her.

She ran.

Fragments

Chapter 7

One week later, Hazel had not seen any more visions of Charlotte, and she had finally gotten some sleep. The staff still talked of her in whispers behind her back—the new writer that saw ghosts around every corner.

She had been staying with Marianne for the last week, ever since she tried to tell Marianne about Charlotte. Marianne was sympathetic to her fears and clear trauma, even if she believed that the ghost was all in Hazel's mind.

Marianne and Hazel had drawn closer to each other, a friendship that deepened each day, and while they didn't speak of it, both women felt the flicker of something awakening in their souls, an initial attraction that went beyond the bounds of friendship and into something much more potent. Marianne calmed Hazel, giving her an anchor when the world became stormy. Hazel excited Marianne, giving her a new lease on life and a purpose outside of acting. The friendship was opposing forces balancing into an equal partnership, and both women secretly felt its pull. With Marianne's red hair and sea-green eyes and Hazel's silver hair and golden eyes, the two were fire and water—an elemental force that overcame anything.

Hazel continued work on her script, but she began to lose her focus as the days passed with no new information. The motive for the murder and the events that occurred after Charlotte was hanged on the stage were still a mystery to her. They were pieces of the puzzle that she needed to be able to complete Charlotte's story.

It would be another two days before Chloe's boss, Daniel, would be able to see them at the theatre. The plan was to wait until the evening's performance was done and let Daniel investigate the dressing room, stage, and foyer. It had all been cleared with Peter under the guise of research and character development for the new play.

***

"A medium, really?" he had said quizzically, an eyebrow arched as he looked suspiciously at the two women in front of him.

He had heard the whispers flying around the staff about Hazel's ghosts.

"Just what is this play about?"

"It's a play about a missing actress and what happened to her. It's a mystery and a love story gone wrong all rolled into one. I just need to know more about her story."

"Why a medium? Is it a horror play? That doesn't sound like it will be popular."

Marianne's voice cut through as she jumped to Hazel's aid. "Peter, look at how popular the runs have been for The *Woman in Black*, *22:22*, and *Ghost Stories*. They've even done multiple tours around the country. People love darker plays."

"It's not a horror play, though." Hazel's voice cracked with frustration. "It's a dark mystery. The medium is here for me to get into her head, that's it."

Marianne looked sheepishly at her and mouthed *I'm sorry*. Hazel nodded to show it was fine, and the two shared a brief smile.

"I just don't know about this, Hazel. It sounds a bit far-fetched." Peter sighed.

"Peter," Marianne began, a lightbulb practically glowing above her head, "you know the woman Hazel is writing about is the woman in the portrait, right? You can use that as your publicity. People want to know about her, about why her portrait was hidden, buried for hundreds of years. Why not sell tickets on the back of that?"

Peter looked at Marianne, a twinkle in his eye as a wry smile tugged at the corner of his mouth.

"Oh, you're good. You should have been in PR. Alright, fine. Write your play, bring in the medium. But if anyone asks, he's a historian and you're just showing him the theatre. Got it?"

"You got it. I promise," Hazel said quickly.

"And if anything happens to jeopardise the reputation of this theatre, you are out on your arse. Do you hear me? Nothing dangerous, nothing stupid."

"Absolutely." Hazel smiled at Marianne.

***

The day before Daniel's visit, the two women were planning on enjoying a lazy Sunday. It was rare that they were both off with Marianne's rehearsal and performance schedule, but today the planets aligned.

Hazel came running into Marianne's room in the morning, brandishing her laptop.

"There's an exhibition of Georgian and Regency artifacts at the British Museum opening today! Can we go?"

Marianne sighed. "What happened to our lazy day?"

"I know, I know. But this could be really useful for me. Please? Come with me." Hazel's bottom lip jutted out in an exaggerated pout, her eyes downcast before quickly meeting Marianne's eyes with a wink.

"Fine! I'll go. But lunch is on you."

"Deal!"

After navigating the crowds on the underground, where all concepts of time and working weeks disappeared in a wave of tourists and those commuters unlucky enough to work in hospitality and retail, they arrived at the British Museum. The grand exterior of the building loomed over them, a columned exterior similar to the theatre. The treasures held inside—some gifted, many collected with love, and many more painful reminders of a history steeped in blood and conquest—ranged from jewellery, artwork, and statues to books, pottery, and clothing.

Hazel and Marianne manoeuvred their way through the queue and past the crowds that thronged the main foyer. Picking their way to the Georgian exhibition, they found themselves steadily walking the length of it, gazing at paintings, clothing, and pottery from the Georgian era. A steady stream of stern faces, hooked noses, and contemptuous sneers loomed from within the ornate frames.

Suddenly, Marianne felt Hazel stiffen beside her, her hand grasping at Marianne's arm with a vice-like grip.

"What is it?" she said quietly.

"Look!" Hazel pointed at the painting to their right.

Princess Caroline of Prussia, Duchess of York, 1754-1810

The princess was seated in a white dress, the satin gleaming on the canvas. Her chocolate-brown, curly hair was piled high on her head, held with a gold ribbon, revealing her graceful neck, which was adorned with a gold and ruby pendant. Her deep-brown eyes looked to the side; her thin lips were pressed together in a slight frown. It was look of kindness, and of melancholy.

"The necklace!" Hazel hissed. "It's the same one!"

The heavy gold chain ended with a pendant of golden squares and embellishments, with rounded rubies adding rich colour. It was the pendant Charlotte was wearing in her portrait.

"Charlotte wore that pendant every day. He made her. He gave it to her, I saw it. He must have stolen it back!"

"Hazel, people are looking. I think you need to calm down," Marianne warned.

Hazel took a deep breath in. "Sorry, I'm calm. But please, listen. She's wearing that exact necklace in the portrait in the theatre. I think he killed her."

"Who?"

"The Duke of York, Frederick. He was obsessed with Charlotte. He followed her everywhere."

"I thought you said she was married?"

"She was, but that didn't stop it. Garrick used her for the patronage. She was powerless."

Marianne fell silent. She recognised the necklace, and she was starting to worry that Hazel was right about everything, including the ghost.

***

The following day, Daniel arrived at the stage door after the evening performance, just as scheduled. Sandy hair and blue eyes on an angular face with thin lips and a small nose gave him a mousy look. He was slight, with the baggy shirt and jeans he wore almost seeming to swallow him. He carried an overnight bag with him that clinked and jolted as he moved.

"Marianne? Hazel?" He gestured at each of them in turn, guessing correctly who was whom.

"That's us. Where would you like to start?"

"I think the portrait seems a good place. Get an idea of her. You said the visitations grew after the portrait was recovered?"

"Yes," Hazel quickly agreed. "I saw her once before, but afterwards she became more physical and started dragging me into her memories."

Ralph raised an eyebrow at the strange visitor being shepherded in after hours with talk of ghosts, but he stayed silent.

Hazel offered him a small smile. "Thanks, Ralph."

He grunted in reply and returned to his book, *From the Stars* by someone called Jim Ody. Ghosts and goblins were not his choice. He preferred crime and sci-fi, and his daughter had just picked up this new release for him that seemed to tick both those boxes. *If I could get a chance to actually read it without all of these interruptions*, he thought.

Hazel and Marianne led Daniel to the dimly lit foyer of the theatre, where Charlotte's portrait was pride of place.

Daniel stepped in front of the painting, reaching out to touch it.

"The sadness in this canvas, it's overwhelming," he whispered. "This is the lady?"

"Charlotte, yes."

"She has dark secrets held in her eyes. They're leaping out at us. How long since you last saw her in the theatre?" he said, still gazing at the painting.

"Just over a week now. I saw her hanging above the stage. We saw that necklace in a painting of the royal family yesterday. I think she was murdered by—"

Daniel raised a hand to stop her before she could finish. "Please, no information that could taint my work." He turned to face Hazel and Marianne. "I can sense a sadness and injustice here, but she is not here. You say it was the stage where you saw her die?"

"Yeah. She was hanging directly above it. I saw her there first as well, before the painting was found. I thought she was a cast member."

"You never told me that," said Marianne quietly. "Daniel, can you tell how long she's been here?"

"If the spirit is Charlotte and the date on the portrait is accurate, she may have been here in one form or another for the entire 250 years."

Hazel's eyes swam. "She must be so lonely."

"But she has also only appeared to Hazel, and reports of this theatre being haunted have been minimal. She may have been dormant until your arrival, Hazel. You seem to be linked with her, whether you like it or not."

A silence settled on the group as Hazel tried to process the idea that a ghostly stranger may have attached to her enough to awaken, while the ghosts she longed for were not there.

"Come on, let's go to the stage and see if I can see her to find out more." Daniel's tone was kind but firm.

Marianne's eyes lingered for a moment on Hazel before she smiled at Daniel and headed through to the auditorium.

As the group reached the stage, Hazel felt an anxious chill through her body. She hadn't been able to shake the image of Charlotte bloody and still, and she wasn't ready to see it again.

Stepping onto the stage, directed by Hazel to the spot where she had been, Daniel gasped. He closed his eyes and held up his hands.

"I can feel her. Fear and pain. There's terror all around us—the air hums with it. A life was taken here, you are right, Hazel. Evil lurks all around us. I'll need to make a paste with salt and holy water to form a protection circle and cleanse the air with burning sage and Paolo Santo to stop this evil from spreading." He began to rummage in his bag for supplies to begin.

Marianne rolled her eyes. She could accept that Hazel might not be completely out of her mind with her wild stories of ghosts and murderous love affairs hundreds of years ago, but the dramatics were a little excessive.

Hazel didn't notice. She had seen a glimmer of movement at the corner of her eye, a flash of red fabric and white hair in the darkness of the stage wing.

"Help me," she heard Charlotte cry in the dark.

"Daniel, there's no time for that, she's over here!" she whispered, pointing towards stage left. Daniel and Marianne followed her gaze as Charlotte appeared again in the gloom, more solidly. She was drifting upwards, as if ascending a staircase that no longer existed. Daniel gasped as Marianne looked blankly into the darkness, unable to see anything.

"She's heading to the rafters. She looks terrified!" Hazel said. "Marianne, do you know how to get up there? We need to follow her."

"I do, it's this way." Marianne led them to the back of the stage, stepping past the backdrop that was hanging in place. In the small corridor created between the canvas and the solid wall of the back of the stage, a small door led to a small staircase that led up to the top of the stage, where the lights and mechanisms for the backdrops were installed. Marianne gestured for them to climb the stairs.

"You go, I'll wait here."

Hurrying up the stairs, Hazel burst into the small balcony that formed the side of the metal bridge system, closely followed by Daniel. Small spotlights stationed along the walkway that ran from one side of the stage to the other lit their way across to a matching balcony above stage right. Above the walkways were the automated pulleys for the backdrops, remotely connected to the board in the tech booth. Large spotlights hung from the sides of the walkway, on motorised arms to achieve perfect lighting angles.

As they gained their bearings, Charlotte appeared in the empty air before them, her eyes slick with tears. She looked frantically over her shoulder as she ran forwards on an unseen walkway, crossing the stage. Her chest heaved as her breaths grew heavy, panic filling her lungs.

Following in parallel, Hazel and Daniel ran across the walkways towards the centre of the stage. Hazel could feel panic and fear rising in her as she followed behind Charlotte.

The dull, steady sound of footsteps behind them made Hazel turn. A dark shadow loomed; the already dark space was made even darker as it moved closer.

Hazel could sense evil—it surrounded her and pressed in on her chest.

"Evil is here. It has come for her," Daniel gasped, his hand once again reaching into his bag to find something to help them. He pulled out a glass bottle filled with a clear liquid.

"Charlotte, run!" Hazel cried.

In the centre of the stage, Charlotte stopped, pulled back by an unseen force.

Voices echoed in the air around them.

"Please don't do this, I've done nothing! Help me, please!"

"Spare your lies, you painted whore. Rot and perish, and be damned."

"Stop—"

The shadow was on them now, moving with an unnatural speed. Daniel jumped in front of Hazel with his arm outstretched, the bottle open as the liquid sprayed out before him. Holy water arced outwardly from Daniel and Hazel, splashing onto the stage below, an attempt to banish the darkness and free Charlotte from the evil presence that held her. There was a shadow of movement, darkness gliding across the pale spotlight and settling across their skin.

There was a small gurgle in front of her, and the walkways cleared. Daniel was gone, a sweep from the shadow sending him flying over the side of the railing and down to the stage. The boards met him with a sickening thud.

Marianne screamed from the stage below.

Charlotte screamed, an echo of Marianne, with her own burden of pain and terror. She dissolved from view.

"Goodbye, Desdemona. May you never know peace for your betrayal," a cruel voice whispered, everywhere and nowhere at once.

The shadow was gone.

Hazel paled, a whimper escaping her as she slowly moved to the side of the walkway. Daniel lay on the stage, his arms bent at unnatural angles where he had tried in vain to break his fall. A pool of blood was spreading, splinters of bone and brain peppering the crimson stain that had been Daniel's now-broken life.

Marianne cried, sobs that racked her as she stared at Daniel's mangled body, unable to move from the shock.

The door burst open, and Ralph appeared, drawn to them by the sounds of screaming.

"What in the bloody hell are you lot up to?"

He stopped as he saw Daniel's corpse.

***

The theatre was closed for the following three months while the police investigated Daniel's death, and the theatre staff recovered. Statements had been taken as Daniel's body was removed that night. The police had naturally been suspicious of Hazel and Marianne as the only witnesses, particularly when Ralph told them that a visitor that late was unusual, and that they had been investigating something strange, but finally they concluded the cause of death was an accidental fall. The official word was that the three were doing a walkaround for historical research, and Daniel had slipped when trying to navigate the bridge on his walkthrough.

Only Hazel knew Daniel had been killed by an evil force haunting the theatre, an echo of history chasing

Charlotte's spirit, a never-ending murder that drew her in and trapped her like a fly in a web.

At home, after taking a couple of weeks off to mourn, Hazel continued writing the play for Charlotte, knowing all the while that Charlotte was trapped in the theatre, running for her life. She felt her connection with Charlotte growing despite the distance.

Her dreams were filled with a constant stream of gold, candlelight, screams, and falling. Daniel's and Charlotte's deaths played on her mind, as well as the fragments of Charlotte's life that she had seen. She heard her voice whispering through each dream.

"Help me."

"Remember me."

"Free me."

Finally, after the three months drew to a close, Hazel finished the final scene of the play. Charlotte was murdered by the Duke of York, his obsession having grown too dark to control. Her body was taken in the dead of night to be buried under the floor of the theatre, never to be found again. She had no proof of it, but Hazel felt in her gut that this scene was Charlotte's fate. The fragments of the story she had seen so far all told her Charlotte would have been kept close by, the theatre that had been her life made her prison in death.

The script was sent to Peter for approval, who reluctantly gave it. Despite the death associated with the play, he knew Marianne was right. This would be popular, now even more so.

Once approved, it was duly emailed to the finalised cast to begin learning their lines, ready for rehearsals to begin as soon as they were back in the theatre.

"Is that this madness over now?" he said in a phone call to Hazel. "No more ghosts and midnight investigations?"

"Maybe one—I want to see the room where the painting was found," she replied.

There was a deep sigh as Peter hung up.

The night the script was finished her dreams changed into something new.

Chapter 8

London, January 1774

Charlotte arrived at the theatre early with James for the opening performance of *Othello*. He always came with her on opening day, even if he couldn't come to the door with her. And now she needed his warm touch more than ever.

"Good luck, my darling. And no matter what happens, I am here with you." He touched her cheek.

"Thank you, my love. I wish that you could be with me today."

"I know, my darling. But your Desdemona will be the talk of the town. I have faith in you. And you have my undying trust and love." He kissed her cheek and walked away, leaving her to approach the stage door alone.

She had thrown her heart and soul into this character, and she was ready. She felt closer to Desdemona than she had even to Ophelia. She now truly understood how dangerous love could be—she felt that twinge of fear whenever Mister York entered the room.

The pendant was heavy around her neck, and despite the fact she wore it every day as she had been directed, she could not get used to it. It was a gold and ruby collar, a chain to remind her she had a master.

She had just made her way to her dressing room when Garrick appeared in the doorway.

"Charlotte, you're here. Good, that was lucky. Your presence has been requested."

She sighed gently, a quiet horror creeping into her stomach, churning and roiling as it settled there.

"Where and by whom?" she asked quietly.

"In my residence. A portrait has been commissioned, one to mark your greatest triumph. You know by whom."

"Why has it been commissioned? I have not sat for a portrait before."

"You have not had such connections before. You have secured the patronage of the theatre from the highest of society and cemented your place as the belle of society. You have done well, Charlotte. The royal family have you in their sights."

"But I do not want this, to be remembered for him. I want to be remembered for my work, not as a courtesan for a wicked man with connections."

Garrick clenched his jaw, gritting his teeth together in anger.

"I will not hear this again. This is not some sordid, tawdry affair. You have done nothing but be a companion, and this hysteria grows tiresome. Make yourself presentable as Desdemona, and present yourself for the initial sketches, please." He turned to go, then paused.

"Oh, and wear the necklace. It has been requested."

Listening to his fading footsteps in the hallway, Charlotte stared at herself in her mirror, an ornate glass gifted to her in replacement of her broken one.

An accident, of course, Garrick had said, smirking, as the shards of silvered glass were swept away, a quiet message for Charlotte that her misery did not matter.

Her thoughts flew, a hundred voices clamouring for attention in her mind.

Will this never end?

What more must I do?

This will not end with a patronage. This will end with blood and gold.

She slowly applied the powder to her face and neck as she quieted the thoughts that tried to overwhelm her, breathing deeply to calm herself. She added rouge to the bones of her cheeks and eyes for colour, and a dark paint on her lips. The red velvet gown that served as her grandest costume in the role came next, the heavy material sliding over her shoulders with a soft caress. Pearls and golden thread adorned the front of the bodice, a perfect match to the pendant that choked her with its worth.

Sweeping her hair over her shoulder, she walked out of the room.

Breathe deeply and well. This will be over soon.

***

The portrait artist gasped as Charlotte entered the room. He had been told of her beauty, but this creature before him had been sent straight from heaven. She was perfect. His mouth opened, awestruck, when a cough from the corner of the room brought him crashing down to earth again.

Dark eyes glittered with a warning.

"Good evening, miss," he said, clearly flustered by her presence. "Please, take a seat here." He gestured at a wooden chair in the centre of the room, accompanied by a table with a candelabra and a vase which held a single red rose.

As Charlotte took her place, she saw the Duke of York, as she now knew him to be, for the first time that evening, seated in the corner of the room. His jaw was set with determination.

"Charlotte, my dear. Thank you for gracing us with your beauty. This portrait will surely be the finest in society. Young Master Hamilton here is very talented. I am ensured he will do his utmost to capture your grace."

Charlotte remained silent, impassive to his words.

The artist, Hamilton, swallowed. "I shall try, my lord. Miss, if you wouldn't mind looking towards me, I shall begin my sketches."

She turned to look at him as silence fell on the room. Her hand instinctively reached up to clasp the necklace, trying to hide the pendant as the pencil scratched on the canvas. The portrait would be perfect, but it would not truly be her with the jewel on display, her silent captor in the room.

Later, as the artist painted alone, he reflected on Charlotte's eyes, grey and blue, as if the sea and sky had come together to bless her, nature itself bowing to her beauty. They had pierced him as she sat there, striking him not only with their force but also with a sense of fear and despair.

"Such sad eyes," he sighed as his brush moved delicately over the canvas.

***

Charlotte left the room as the sketch concluded as quickly as she was able to. The day was drawing to a close, and the performance would soon begin. Desdemona would be unveiled to the world, a perfect victim and beautiful damsel in distress.

She stood in the hallway for a moment, stretching her arms and legs, her limbs warming to movement as she slowly loosened them. Her pose had been as comfortable as possible, but still her body resisted her now.

She was only a few steps away when Mister York strode from the room in pursuit. Holding her arm, he stopped her mid-step.

"Charlotte," he began, maintaining a grip on her arm, "I must know something from you."

"Your grace?"

"I saw you earlier. With a man. I watched him kiss your cheek. It seemed—intimate. I must know who he is."

Charlotte's breath caught in her throat.

"He is nothing to concern yourself about, your grace. A relative."

"If I thought that someone held your affection more than I—" The sentence was left unfinished, the threat clear as his grip on her arm tightened, sending shooting pains up to her shoulder.

"Please, I must insist that you release me. I am needed elsewhere." The strength in her tone masked the fear and pain coursing through her.

Releasing her arm, he placed his hand under her jaw, forcing her to meet his eye. There was a pause, his thin lips pressed together in a grimace. Finally, his hand moved to the pendant around her neck.

"Don't forget how much I can give. And how much I can take away."

She turned away, tears welling in her eyes, the pain in her arm throbbing as a reminder of his strength.

"I must go."

He watched her walk away, an uneasy feeling in his gut. A quiet fury raged that he struggled to control. She brought it out in him, a force that ignored his military discipline and set his soul ablaze. If she was not faithful to him, he would see to it that both were punished.

If he couldn't have her, no man would.

***

She moved through the scenes with grace and a quiet dignity that the audience was captivated by. Her connection with the character made her become Desdemona. They ached for her, wept for her, shared in her joys, and mourned her end. Cries for justice echoed in their hearts even as they were rooted to their seats in rapt silence.

Garrick met her eye as she moved to the centre of the stage for her curtain call. Pride was etched in every line on his face as he presented her to the audience.

Roses littered her feet as she looked out over the adoring crowd. This was truly her moment in the sun.

In the royal box, he sat by his brother George, the Prince of Wales, as the new patrons of the theatre. Their arrival in the box that evening had caused a rolling tide of whispers, the women of society jostling for attention. Both princes looked resplendent in military dress, and they returned the attention with sweeping, gracious looks. Small, impassive gestures were enough for them.

Now, it was all forgotten.

"She is magnificent, is she not, brother?" the duke hissed at the Prince of Wales through the applause.

"I can see why she has enchanted you. Talented and beautiful, without a doubt, and this company is worth the patronage. But be warned, brother, this is not a match you should pursue, and I will oppose it. Your marriage to Princess Caroline is almost set. That is the creature to whom you should address your affections." He glanced at the actress taking her bow.

"And your jewellery."

"Princess Caroline is a malignant horse of a woman, and I will not be bound to her when this radiant creature is before me. She will be mine, brother, whatever you have to say. I shall have my way."

"She is an actress. Do you not see that any affection she shows is mere pretence? An affectation? You are blinded by her beauty, brother. You are a prince of the realm, and you will not debase yourself by consorting with a peasant, however popular she may be."

Prince George rose to his feet, offered a nod of his head to the company assembled on stage patiently waiting for his approval, and vacated the box.

Prince Frederick met Charlotte's gaze from the stage and smiled as he took his leave behind his brother. She looked away quickly, her eyes moving over the crowd, as her hand caressed her arm.

The gold pendant glittered in the glow of the stage lights.

***

Returning to her dressing room, Charlotte smiled at the memory of the adoring audience—the thunderous applause, the flowers, and the pure love that had radiating to her from the crowd.

As she entered the room, the smile on her face fell. On the dressing table was a single rose with a note.

You are mine above all others. I will never let you go. -F

A shuddering sob freed itself from deep within her.

Chapter 9

London, 2025

Hazel awoke from her dream with a start. She could still hear the applause thundering in her memory, see the flicker of the lamps, and feel the tension from the royal box.

The day the theatre was due to open for backstage staff, ready to start preparations for the new play, Hazel found herself holding her breath as she walked through the stage door. For the first time since her induction, she had no idea what to expect as she entered the theatre.

Ralph was back at his post, the shock of Daniel's death still lining his face. Deep, dark circles underneath his eyes told Hazel everything she needed to know about the traumatic dreams that must plague his nights.

"Hi, Ralph. How are you?" she asked sincerely.

"I don't know if I'm ready for this, Wilkins. I don't know if I have it in me anymore, not after that." He sighed, weary of the world. He seemed smaller than before, and she could see the pain in him.

"Do you need to take more time? Surely someone else can take over for you?"

"I need to be here. You'll understand more than anyone what it's like, to see him every time you close your eyes. I need to stay busy."

Hazel paused. She had been focussed on Charlotte and her play; she had almost forgotten the dreams of Daniel. Feeling guilty, she nodded, placed a reassuring hand on Ralph's shoulder, and carried on into the theatre.

As she reached her office, Peter was waiting for her. He looked haggard, stress marking his face. Thin lips clenched as he forced his way through pleasantries. There was something on his mind.

"Hazel, how are you? Ready to be back?"

"Peter, hi. I'm good, thanks. Definitely happy to be out of my flat. How are you doing?"

"Well, the stage looks good. You would never know what—" He paused, unable to get the words out.

Hazel nodded reassuringly.

"And what about the preparations?" she asked, tying to change the subject.

"Well, we have the lighting sorted from the script prompts. The staging needs some work, and the joiners need to work on the drop mechanism for the hanging in the finale. I'm just a little—concerned."

"About what?"

"The ending. Buried in the theatre? The last thing we need is a rumour like that. You tell everyone that she's buried down there and we'll have ghosthunters and loonies swarming the stage door."

"What are you asking me to do?"

"Change it. Have her thrown in the river, something away from the theatre."

"But that's not what I—"

"I don't care. Hazel, I have to insist on this. I don't ask for much, but considering everything that's happened lately, you'll excuse me for thinking of the theatre before your ghost story. You are on thin ice, and I can't let—no, *won't* let this play jeopardise us. You'll send the changes to me today to distribute to the cast before they come to that scene."

Hazel nodded, her eyes downcast. He was right; everything wrong with the theatre had been because of her chasing ghosts. Her stories.

"Alright, I'll do it. But please, let me see the store room where the painting was found. I need to know."

"The play first, then we'll talk. This whole thing is absolute lunacy. You need to see someone about this, Hazel. A professional." As he said this, he strode out the door and out of sight.

She sat in her office, the script swimming in front of her eyes. The ending didn't feel right. Charlotte deserved more than being thrown into the river, sinking into the cold, black depths of the Thames.

As she typed the new ending, she could feel Charlotte's presence enter the room, the cold air pricking at Hazel's skin. She could feel goosebumps forming on her arms, as if guarding her body against a winter chill.

"I have to do this, Charlotte. I hope you understand," she said to the empty room as she finished the final line and saved the second draft.

The peace of the room was shattered by a scream that echoed through Hazel's brain, taking her breath away.

There was the sound of glass breaking as the window imploded, sending shattered glass flying into the room under the force of the anguished cry. Hazel covered her ears as she ducked behind the desk, shaking.

"Find me."

Silence fell on the room as Hazel removed her hands from her ears and peeked out from behind the desk.

The window was unbroken.

Find me.

***

Rehearsals were underway. Marianne in the role of Charlotte had captured her beautifully, whether she knew it or not. Her nuanced reading was demure yet captivating. She commanded the stage, but captured the fear and helplessness Hazel had tried to instil in the script. Russell Halliwell, the new male lead for the season, had captured the haughty demeanour of the Duke of York, creating a threatening air and tension that followed him into the scenes like a silent storm. An experienced actor, Russell had tuned in to the entitled attitude of the duke even when silent. *I want, so I shall have.*

As rehearsals progressed, Hazel became less and less aware of Charlotte's presence in the theatre, but she seemed to see the shadows move and darken. The entity that killed Daniel was there and growing stronger.

It was during the first full rehearsal of the finale that she knew it was him.

It was a scene they had rehearsed the stunt for multiple times, but not the scene itself: newly changed to show Charlotte's murder at the hand of the Duke of York before her body was taken to the river and left to sink into a watery grave. The harness used to support Marianne during the hanging had been carefully made to measure and fit her snugly underneath her costume, a red gown to match the portrait in the lobby. She stood on the drop platform on a false walkway that had been built, lower than the original to remain in the view of the audience, preparing herself for the drop. However safely it was performed, and no matter how many times she did the stunt, it jarred her, and she found herself nervous each time.

Russell was beside her. His cloak, hat, and a simple black mask completed his transformation into the malicious shadowy killer, who would be revealed to the audience.

As Marianne was buckled into the harness, they performed the stunt, her ribs crying out with the jolt from the harness. As she swung in the air, simulating death by hanging, the scene continued.

"Goodbye, Desdemona. May you never know peace for your betrayal."

He removes hat and mask, looks to audience.
Exit stage right.

Bang!

Russell fell to the stage from the false walkway, a flash of light blinding the cast and crew assembled for a moment. A crackling noise could be heard in the quiet.

A stage light, fallen from the walkway far above them—the same walkway from which the shadowy figure had thrown Daniel—lay on the stage beside Russell. Exposed wires left behind where the light had ripped away from its bracket crackled with live energy above them.

"Russell!"

"Are you alright?"

"What happened up there?"

Voices clamoured as cast and crew rushed to Russell's side. Still winded from his fall, he began to sit up, cradling his left arm where the falling light had clipped it.

"That could have killed you! Is it broken?" Marianne cried, undoing the final buckle on her harness and bracing for a small drop to the stage, desperate to go to him.

"I don't think so," he said, gingerly stretching his arm. "Just badly bruised, I think. Can someone get me some ice, for fuck's sake?"

Hazel felt the hairs on her arms stand on end, as if she was being watched. She looked up at the walkway. A dark shadow loomed above them, quiet and menacing, before disappearing towards the darkened wing beside stage right. As the shadow disappeared, the sparking lights from the live cables died, cut off by the circuit breaker, leaving nothing but silence from the walkway above. Lit only by the spotlights and house lights, an eerie glow fell on Russell, his face white from shock.

Peter appeared on the stage, his face ashen. His once kind face had taken on a hollowed look, his kind eyes sombre and glassy.

"Russell, are you alright?"

"What kind of cowboys have you got in this place, Warner? I could have been killed!"

Marianne placed a hand on Russell's right shoulder. "Russell, it was an accident. It's not his fault. Come on, we need to get you checked out at the hospital." She gave Hazel a long, pointed look before helping Russell to his feet, along with Peter.

Hazel watched them go as the rest of the crew disappeared to the staff rooms.

Rehearsals were over.

***

Hazel wandered the theatre, her thoughts on the shadow. She knew that if more accidents plagued them Peter would shut down the play, and Charlotte would never be free.

She soon found herself in the lobby, looking at the locked door which led towards the basement.

"I'll find you, Charlotte, I will." Her promise echoed in the empty foyer. She hadn't seen Charlotte since Daniel's death and hadn't felt her since she changed the ending for the play. Worry sat within her, a stone that weighted her to the floor.

What if I'm too late to help her?

A sudden chill fell over the room as laughter echoed in the air—deep and cruel. The shadow Hazel had come to fear flitted over the staircase, moving towards her. As it passed over the painting of Charlotte, the portrait's painted skin turned to bone, hair to ash, lips shrank to nothing, those glistening eyes melted down hollow, hardened cheeks. The sweet yet acrid smell of rot hung in the air.

The malevolent shape moved closer to Hazel, and as it did, the portrait returned to its former state, rich and vibrant, full of life.

Remembering Daniel and his blood and bone scattered across the stage, Hazel turned and fled from the darkness. The malicious laugh pounded in her head, growing louder as the shadow approached. Passing her by, she stopped and watched as it moved through the locked door and out of sight.

A harsh whisper lingered in the air.

"She will never know freedom."

Hazel stared at the door with bated breath as silence fell over the room. Her breath misted in the air as she released it, but she felt the warmth returning to her bones.

The evil spirit made of shadow and darkness would not let the play go ahead.

She needed to get into that basement, and soon.

Chapter 10

Hazel sat in her office, her fingers furiously sweeping over the keys of her laptop. Charlotte would not be free unless Hazel could get rid of, or at least trap, the evil shadow that meant her harm.

After frantic searches on types of spirits and the nature of hauntings, she found herself on a message board for paranormal researchers, mediums, and spiritualists.

How do I trap an evil spirit that causes harm? Hazel typed into the message board. A flurry of replies soon appeared on the screen.

-Burn sage for cleansing the air. Or Paolo Santo. Or both. Herbs are your friend! Good luck.

*

-Try a circle of salt to bind it.

*

-You need an old priest and a young priest.

-STFU troll. This is a serious board.

-Yeah? Well, so's your mum. Frigid.

-Let's fucking go.

*

-Iron or silver should keep evil spirits at bay.

-I thought that was just on Supernatural?

-See if they can help! So hot.

-Hey, they did their research. It really does work, as long as the metal is pure.

-If I had those boys around, nothing would be pure.

*

-Holy water will hurt it.

-Use salt and HW, hit it with both.

*

-If you want to banish it, trap it in salt and tell it to leave.

-You want her to tell it off? Can I have some of whatever you've been smoking?

-No, she's right. Yell at it!

-Be firm, and don't ask. Tell it to leave, it will have to, eventually.

*

Her thoughts flew back to Daniel's fateful visit to the theatre and the kit he had brought with him.

Evil lurks all around us. I'll need to make a paste with salt and holy water to form a protection circle, and cleanse the air with burning sage and Paolo Santo to stop this evil from spreading.

"Well, Daniel, I guess you were on to something, there," she said aloud.

Unable to bring herself to go to Daniel's shop, she managed to purchase the Paolo Santo incense and sage bundle from an online wiccan site. The salt she could get at the local corner shop. Silver she had at home. Her parents had owned a set of two Victorian candlesticks made from antique silver. Pure. After their deaths, Hazel had prized these heirlooms more than anything, and they now sat pride of place on her bedroom bureau, even if they didn't fit in with her more modern décor.

That just left the holy water. St. Paul's wasn't far away. Known as *The Actor's Church*, they were used to dramatic worshippers and big events. Many actors, writers, and directors had sat in its pews, praying for their debut to go well or for that dream part to come their way, selfish prayers for the talented few with a dream, and no possibility of failure.

As the day drew to a close, Hazel stepped inside the church. A sign of the times, of religion slowly dying, she was alone. Even in a vibrant and busy part of London, no worshippers had come to the church for prayer or guidance.

She sat for a moment in a wooden pew in the nave, facing the altar. She could see the baptismal font in an alcove on her left, tucked away towards the front of the hallowed building. As she sat, she thought of everything she had experienced since beginning her work at the theatre. The deaths of Daniel and of Charlotte, the dreams that stopped her from rest, the hallucinations, all of it. She wept quietly, mourning the life and job that she had wanted, now twisted into something she no longer recognised. She mourned for her loss as much as she did for Daniel and Charlotte. And she mourned for her parents, the spirits she would give anything to see, not this shadowed evil that followed her through her days.

As she wept, soft footsteps echoed through the space behind her. A priest with a kind face, his black robe swishing with each step, approached her. He looked to be in his early sixties, with greying brown hair and soft features, large eyes that creased at the edges from a life of laughter and smiles, a button nose, and a thin mouth that drooped slightly downwards, giving him a naturally sympathetic expression.

"Why do you weep, my child? May I be of any help to you?"

"I don't think anyone can help me, Father. Do you believe in ghosts?" The priest looked confused.

"I believe in the spirit, in the soul. Is that what you mean?"

"Do you believe the spirit, the soul, can stay after you die?"

"Well, not in the sense of things that go bump in the night. Demons, yes, but not ghosts and ghouls."

Hazel dropped her gaze to the floor.

"A ghost needs my help, and a ghostly shadow follows me. I'm scared, Father, and no one really believes me."

"My child, what makes you think that?"

"I've seen things, heard things. A man is dead! Everywhere I look, I see spirits, and I see fragments of a life that wasn't mine to see. The good spirit and the evil spirit are both plaguing me, and I don't know what to do."

"Good and evil have always been at war. Our souls are the battlefield, our lives and actions the weapons. Remember, sometimes evil hides behind a façade of goodness. Evil may trick, manipulate, and lie under a face of purity and love with sweetened words that carry poison to our minds and hearts. The greatest evil that we must face may rest inside ourselves and those we love and trust."

"I know the difference in these spirits, Father."

"Then it is simple. True goodness reveals itself in thought, word, and action. Only you and the Almighty above can know what direction your life will take. What choice do you see before you?"

"I can help the good spirit and maybe the evil spirit will kill me, maybe it won't. Or I can walk away and chalk this whole thing up to me going mad."

"And which of these choices does your heart feel is right?"

She sighed. "I need to help her. I have to be there for Charlotte. Can I ask you for something?"

"Of course, my child. What do you need?"

"May I take some of your holy water from the font?"

The priest looked at the font, then back to her. In his mind, he hoped this poor lost soul would seek help from a psychiatrist, but her pleading eyes had him caught.

"Do what you must, and go with my blessing."

She thanked him and headed to the font, where she slowly filled an empty bottle with the sacred liquid. As she turned to go, the priest called to her from the pew where he had stayed behind.

"My child?"

"Yes, Father?"

With his arm outstretched, he made the sign of the cross in the air before her.

"May the lord watch over and keep you. Be safe, my child, and may you find the answers you seek."

***

Russell was back the following day, his arm recovered enough to gently work his way through a rehearsal.

His understudy was constantly crossing the boundary between relieved and disappointed at Halliwell's recovery, hovering at the edge of the stage as the rehearsal continued.

Seated in the stalls, Hazel passed the day in a daze, her mind purely on the supplies she had ordered, which were due for delivery any day. With opening night only two nights away, every hour counted.

As the play's first half came to an end, Peter appeared beside her in the stalls. They sat quietly for a moment before he spoke.

"Why do you want to go to the basement so eagerly?"

"I need to see it, Peter. I need to see if there's any sign of her in that sealed room."

He sighed. "It goes against my better judgement, and I think you are in serious need of psychiatric help if you expect to find ghosts down there. But, if it will help you see sense, I am willing to try."

He held out a key.

She took it from his outstretched hands and nodded.

"Thank you, Peter. I know you don't believe me. Hell, I wouldn't believe me. But I need this."

"I have one demand, Hazel. The renovation team needs to be with you for safety and security. Tom and Scott are waiting for you. At least one of them has to go down there with you."

"Okay. Seriously, thank you for this."

Peter nodded in response.

Hazel picked her way out of the row of seats and headed towards the side exit of the auditorium. On her way to the locked door by the foyer that led to the basement, she stopped at the small staff kitchen, where she found a small container of salt that she slipped into her trouser pocket.

Making her way to the door, she spotted two men standing in the hallway, looking expectantly in each direction. A tall, younger man who looked to be in his

twenties, with dark skin, curly, black hair, and brown eyes saw her approaching and turned to his companion, a middle-aged white man with a slight pot belly and brown hair streaked with grey. He indicated her approach, and they turned to face her.

"You Hazel Wilkins?" the older man asked.

"That's me. Are you Tom and Scott, from the renovation team?"

"Yeah, I'm Scott," the younger of the two said, before gesturing to the older man.

"This is Tom. He's the team supervisor."

"That I am." Tom stepped forwards. "Now, do you want to tell us what we're doing here, when the work was halted?"

"Didn't Peter tell you?"

"He told us we were to take you down there. I want to know what for."

"The room you found, the one that was sealed up with the painting. Was there anything else in there?"

"I think there were some props," Scott said. "But to be honest, we just grabbed the painting and left."

"We're not archaeologists, Miss Wilkins," Tom added. "It was above our pay grade to look at the place more than we did."

"Well, I need to see it now. I think there might be something else in there. Something important."

"I doubt there's anything there," Tom said, a raised eyebrow, showing the scepticism he felt. "But if we're going in there, you'll need these. It's still a building site." He held up a pack, which Hazel took. Inside was a hard hat, a high-vis vest, a torch, and a radio.

After putting on the equipment, she unlocked the door. A blast of cold air met her as she stepped into the darkened doorway beyond, her torch shining a small circle of light ahead of her. A small corridor led to a narrow set of steps descending into the bowels of the theatre.

Slowly, she moved forwards, listening for the slightest sound as her torch beam swept over the stairs.

A small voice whispered in her ear, a disembodied call.

"Find me."

"I will. I'm coming," she replied to the empty dark.

"What?" came a voice behind her on the stairs. Tom was following her closely, and she could hear Scott in the hallway above, making his way towards them.

"Nothing, it's nothing. Let's go."

As she and Tom in turn stepped onto solid ground from the bottom step, a black shape glanced over the beam of light from the torch, heading around the two at the bottom of the stairs. It reflected nothing, absorbing the light into a black pit of despair and emptiness.

"No!" she gasped. Following the shadow with the light, she saw it snake up the steps and towards Scott.

"What is it?" said Tom, his eyes flickering to Hazel with a confused expression. He flipped a switch on the wall, and the room filled with a dim light.

There was a crunching sound, and the step beneath Scott's left foot gave way. Losing his balance, he pitched forwards, falling down the remaining steps. His head, arms, and legs hit off each step with a sharp smacking noise before he landed in a heap at the bottom of the stairs.

"Scott!" Tom shouted, rushing to the foot of the stairs. "Are you alright?"

Hazel heard a small laugh echoing from the stairs. It was him.

Scott groaned as he pulled himself up from the ground, stretching his arms and legs gingerly as he tested the bones and joints.

"Just bruised, I think. Christ, that hurt!" he said, rubbing the back of his neck.

Tom helped him to his feet, checking him over for any wounds.

"You're alright, mate. Good thing you were wearing your hard hat, though, that took the worst of it. You just need a bit of rest. Do you want to go back upstairs?"

"I think I probably should. Can you help me?"

Tom looked at Hazel. "I'll be back in a minute. Don't touch anything, okay?"

She nodded, her eyes still on the staircase. As the two men disappeared into the hallway above, she retrieved the salt from her pocket, sprinkling a handful over the stairs. It was time to put this lore to the test. And time to move forwards.

The dimly lit room loomed before her. Construction materials and equipment lay scattered across the floor. Lining the walls beside original fireplaces were small, broken inner walls that formed the original parts of the theatre. Bookcases and shelves filled with cardboard storage boxes and labelled files were covered in cobwebs. This was an archaeological site, building site, and storeroom all rolled into one. Looking at the labels on the files, she could make out a variety of documents.

Theatre Plans
Costume Directories
Material Swatches
Scripts 1980-1999

Scripts 2000-2020
Scripts 2021-

The final box was the only one not covered in dust, the surface of the shelf newly buffed where someone had dragged the box on and off the shelf recently.

A set of tattered, red velvet stall seats rested in a corner, silent witnesses to countless performances, now reduced to a home for spiders and dust.

At the edge of the room sat a brick wall with a telltale hole, just large enough for a person to climb through. She crossed the room and placed her hand on the wall.

"Here. Always here." A gentle voice carried across the room.

Hazel sighed, a small smile crossing her face. She was so close.

"What are you doing?" a booming voice came from the stairs. Tom had returned. "Didn't I say not to touch anything?"

Hazel jerked her hand away from the wall, brick dust falling to the ground as she did.

"Sorry, I didn't think—"

"This is a building site. You have to be careful. The brickwork could be loose, for all you know." His voice was stern.

"I'm sorry. Is Scott alright?"

"He'll be sore for a few days, but nothing's broken. Strange, that step was never weak before."

"Things have been strange everywhere in the theatre since you found this room. Can I go in?"

Tom clenched his jaw. He tested the wall for any loose stones that might make it unstable. Finding nothing, he looked at her. "Alright, let's get this over with. Do you need help getting through there?"

"What are you going to do, push my arse?" She smirked as Tom's face flushed scarlet. Holding her torch aloft with one hand and using the other to balance, she swung a leg over the wall beneath the hole and shimmied her way through to the room beyond.

Moving quickly, she created a line of salt at the base of the wall. If it worked, the shadow wouldn't be able to breach the room.

The room beyond was small. The floor consisted of loose, unbalanced floorboards that felt somehow soft, covered with dust and earth, and it had solid stone walls. A trail of footprints in the dust and dirt led to an old trunk resting by the outer wall. Beside it lay a pile of linen cloth, carelessly discarded, and a sword and goblet. Props of no real value, glass jewels glinting in the torch light.

Picking up the cloth and shaking off the dust, it seemed to be a large handkerchief. Once a pale colour, it was marked with large patches of rusty-brown stains.

Blood.

She could make out initials on the cloth, picked out in a pale thread that might once have held a golden hue. The initials read *F.A.Y* with a small crest.

"Frederick Augustus of York. So it was you."

A rustling noise from the back wall was the only reply.

Moving her attention to the trunk, Hazel looked at the lock—rusted through. With a sharp hit from her torch, it popped open with ease.

Tom peered through the hole behind her.

"Everything okay in there?"

"Yeah, fine. I'm just looking in this trunk."

A loud banging noise from the basement behind her drew her attention.

"Tom, are you alright?" she called.

He quickly appeared at the hole in the wall, his face pale.

"One of the bookcases just toppled. That scared the crap out of me! I don't know what happened—they were sturdy!"

"Are you hurt?"

"No, I'm alright."

"I think something doesn't want me looking here. Why don't you come in here with me? There's enough space if I shuffle up."

He didn't need to be told twice and quickly hopped over the wall, missing the salt line by a hair's breadth. He had a chill running up his spine that he didn't want to admit to. Something about this place gave him the feeling they weren't alone. Peter had warned him that Hazel had wild stories and ideas, but something about her ghosts rang true.

"Help me with this trunk lid, it's heavy."

They lifted the lid, and it fell against the stone wall with a resounding thud.

The sweet smell of flowers met them, a smell Hazel knew but couldn't place.

Red velvet lay carefully folded, still full of colour after all this time locked away. She lifted it up, revealing a rich, red velvet dress, heavy and luxurious. A decorative golden comb lay beneath it on the bottom of the trunk. This was Charlotte's costume. Suddenly she placed that floral smell, the ghost of which lingered on the fabric. Roses and honey.

Charlotte's perfume.

She staggered, feeling lightheaded.

Tom grabbed her before she lost her balance.

"Hazel, are you alright?"

She groaned. "Just a bit dizzy. I'll be al—"

The sentence died in her throat as her attention was caught by something on the other side of the room. Out of sight from the hole where they had come in, tucked into the right, was a patch of floor that seemed to be a darker colour than the rest.

"Hazel?"

"Tom, have you got a broom and shovel out there by any chance?" she asked, never breaking her gaze from the floor.

"Probably, why? What are you doing?"

"Look, there." She pointed at the patch in the floor. "There's something there."

Tom glanced nervously at the hole, the feeling of being watched returning. "Okay, but what if more shelves topple?"

As if in response, there was a loud crash from outside.

Hazel reached into her pocket for the salt. Bringing out the container, her stomach dropped.

It was empty.

"We'll go together. Watch the salt line when you're crossing—we need that." She pointed at the thin white line at the base of the wall.

"I didn't see that. What have you done that for?"

"Whatever's out there, do you want it in here with us? That stops it—it's trapped in the basement and getting angry. But I'm out of salt, so we've got to be quick. Where would the broom and shovel be?"

He nodded in understanding as he gestured to the far right of the basement, by the stairs. He wasn't sure how he had gotten there, with a poltergeist throwing a tantrum and a dark treasure hunt in the ruins of an old theatre, but there he was. And Hazel seemed confident, like she knew exactly what to do. He kind of liked that about her—the quiet, sweet exterior melting away to a confident, strong woman. His wife had been like that, before the divorce. He missed her. Over time, the memory of arguments and poisoned words faded, leaving him with only a sense of loss and nostalgia.

"Are you ready?"

Hazel's voice plucked him out of his thoughts, and he looked through the hole at the basement, then at her. "Ready."

He climbed through the hole, followed by Hazel. The air was dense, a solid mass that pressed down on their lungs, making each breath feel as if it was a million miles away. The shelves wobbled and moved, the contents of boxes strewn over the floor, a jumble of papers, fabric, and blueprints.

He pointed to the far side of the basement, beside the staircase. A metal cabinet occupied the space against the side of the wooden steps.

"That's where they should be, in there." He stepped towards the metal cabinet and disappeared from Hazel's eyeline as a red shape collided with him.

"Tom!" she cried, rushing forwards. He lay on the floor by the side of the stairs, crumpled. A pool of blood slowly spread from a wound at his right temple, his eyes fluttering as he swam in and out of consciousness. His arm lay at a strange angle that could only mean dislocation or a break. A tattered theatre chair, ripped from its metal support, lay on the ground beside him.

The shadow waited, laughing, it's shape growing to fill the basement completely.

Hazel was surrounded, a black fog of malice coating her skin and crushing her bones.

The darkness moved across her eyes, and as it did, she saw a glimmer of white. The world smelled faintly of roses and honey.

Her eyes closed as consciousness slipped away.

Fragments

Chapter 11

London, March 1774

Charlotte and James walked hand in hand through the street beside their modest house. It was a beautiful spring day with a light, refreshing rain that coated their skin like a fine veil of cool silk. Charlotte relished these days.

Over the past few months, she had grown thinner, her skin even paler against the dark hollows that pronounced her bones through her skin. Her eyes were slightly dimmer than before, a haunted nature to them that few could ignore. Her beauty remained, but it was plain to see she carried a great burden that wasted her.

Her Desdemona was the talk of the city, the season a sell-out, and the patronage of the theatre was secure. The duke had been summoned to Prussia, leaving Charlotte blissfully alone and free to be with James. When she was with James, the light returned to her eyes, the glow to her skin. She radiated joy in the spring showers.

She heard rumours the duke was to be betrothed to Princess Caroline of Prussia, and her heart leapt at the idea that he may return with a wife to place his attentions on instead. He had been sullen and withdrawn for the last few weeks at the thought of leaving, but she hoped with everything she was that the engagement would be announced. If it was, she may be able to sever herself from this imprisonment of her life. She felt like today she and James could venture further on their walk, safe and free.

Lost in her thoughts, Charlotte felt a tug on her hand. James had turned to look at her, his eyes filled with love, longing, and sorrow all at once. He had seen her wilt away before his eyes, helpless to stop the play that was set in motion in their lives.

"Charlotte, my love, are you alright?"

"I am fine. Really, I am. Today I feel—happy. Finally, everything seems to be in our favour. I love you."

They kissed, a long, deep kiss that pulled their souls together into one. The world around them fell away, a silent observer of their love.

A man walking up the street behind them stopped, his eyes trained on the couple. A nervous expression on his face as he twirled his moustache, he turned and hurried away in the opposite direction.

"Miss Robinson!" a voice called.

Jolted from their moment of blissful solitude, Charlotte turned to find Mrs Lilian Thomas, a society belle, with her trusted companions, Mrs Bell and Mrs Whitcombe. All three ladies were young brides who had quickly climbed the ranks of society, eventually finding themselves in the company of the Queen herself. All three were blonde, with blue eyes and small features that made them look younger still. Lilian was the leader of the group, her radiant smile and sparkling wit always the centre of the room. Kathryn Bell and Lydia Whitcombe always fell in line behind, quiet and unassuming, but always watching and listening.

As the trio approached, the smile Charlotte reserved for society and the general public—one that didn't quite meet her eyes—appeared on her lips.

"Mrs Thomas, Mrs Bell, Mrs Whitcombe. How delightful to see you!" she exclaimed, the enthusiasm in her voice disguising the exhaustion and derision she felt.

"Lovely to see you Miss Robinson, if only 'twere not such a miserable day."

"Do you not find the rain most refreshing? I love the spring." Charlotte smiled gently.

"I find that I should enjoy it more were I a flower. I, however, need nourishment of a different nature and prefer my skin to remain dry." Her two companions nodded enthusiastically at this. Lilian continued as if they weren't even there.

"We were on our way to a luncheon, but how fortuitous it is that we should meet you here, Miss Robinson. Your performance last night was simply divine. I could not imagine a more perfect victim."

Charlotte swallowed at the veiled insult she knew had just been delivered.

"Thank you, Mrs Thomas. It is always so gratifying to know that my performances are being so highly lauded by those with such a rich understanding of the plight of an unhappy woman."

A slight scowl flashed across Lilian's face, as her two companions widen their eyes. Rumours of her husband's infidelity and harsh temper were rife in society, but few would draw attention to it in front of her.

With Lilian's eyes fixed on her, Charlotte felt heat rising up her body as her smile began to waver. She looked away, flashing a small look at James to steel herself.

Lilian's eyes followed her gaze, settling on James.

"It is good to see you enjoying your day away from the theatre. And who is your companion?"

"My husband, James." Charlotte spoke without thinking, the heat from the exchange of insults still coursing through her. She felt James stiffen beside her as the three ladies looked shocked.

"Husband? Well, fancy that. You have been keeping secrets, *Mrs* Robinson." She emphasised Charlotte's name, letting it roll over her tongue before spitting it out into the world.

"I—well—" Charlotte stammered, unable to find the words.

"Well, we mustn't keep you in the rain, and we shall be late for luncheon. It was truly a pleasure to see you. Most enlightening. Goodbye, Mr Robinson, Mrs Robinson." The trio glided away, their delicate whispers carrying on the breeze.

"What have I done?" Charlotte whispered.

***

The duke returned to his London residence alone. His temper was foul, a dark cloud of anger and malice following him in his wake.

His spy left behind to keep watch over Charlotte had witnessed her kissing a man with a great deal of passion on the street and reported it immediately. He had seemed in great pain delivering the message, nervously tugging on his moustache as if fearful it would be ripped from his lip. Which it nearly was.

The duke met this news with a violent rage, raining blows down on the man with an iron candlestick. The messenger's bloodied face unrecognisable, his breath faint, Frederick coldly ordered him to be dumped by the river. The London night would take him.

The man in the street, he knew that description. He had seen that same man near the theatre with Charlotte. She had lied to him.

Darkness settling in his eyes, he stormed into the night. He would find him, no matter what.

***

Charlotte heard whispers wherever she went, the revelation of James too big a story not to share. By the time she arrived at the theatre the following day, it seemed all of London knew of James and her secret life.

Garrick was waiting for her when she arrived at her dressing room.

"What in hell's teeth have you done, girl?" he spat, his teeth clenched together in anger, his jaw hard.

"It was an accident. But I am glad of it. I am tired of hiding James in the shadows, of hiding my life. Let the world know him, and let the duke be damned. He has his Prussian princess; he has no need of me." Her voice rose though she remained calm.

A flash of pity broke through his anger.

"My poor child, you have had to hide so much from the world, and I know better than any man how painful that is." A glimmer of understanding flickered in his face. "But do you have any idea what you have done? Frederick does not forgive, and he does not forget."

"If he truly cares for me, he should want my happiness above all else."

"You know nothing of the real world, you stupid, naïve child. His pride means more to him than your happiness, and you know it. You have taken a great risk here, Charlotte. And you or I will pay for it."

"I have already paid for it, Garrick, with my silence and my company these past months."

With a scowl, Garrick left.

The performance that evening was as glorious as ever. The venomous Iago, perfect and pure Desdemona, and the brooding Othello were all visions of perfection. The spellbound audience met the end of the play with thunderous applause, their cheers giving each of the company a warm glow that settled in their hearts and wouldn't let go.

Charlotte's adoring public greeted her at the stage door with notes of congratulations on her apparent recent marriage. Looks of disappointment that she was lost to the hopeful masses soon faded when she appeared with gracious smiles and warm affection.

Reaching her home that evening, Charlotte was surprised to see the lanterns unlit. James usually waited for her homecoming, eager to hear about her performance that evening.

Has he fallen ill? she thought, hurrying to the door that led to their kitchen. It sat ajar, the evening breeze causing it to sway slightly. She knew in her gut something was wrong.

"James?" she called, pushing the door open fully and cautiously glancing around the darkened room. There was no reply.

Lighting the lantern by the door, she could see a chair had been upturned, lying on its side beside a fallen plate swept from the table. Crumbs of bread and the remains of a stew lay on the floor.

Mixed with the brown stew were spots of a deep-red liquid that Charlotte couldn't bring herself to look at.

Blood.

"James?" she called again and again, searching through each room in turn. The house was empty.

James was gone.

***

Two days later, James had not appeared. The March winds were drawing on, bringing April in their wake, and still no sign. Charlotte had searched everywhere she could think of.

Her performances of Desdemona had altered as her mind drifted with thoughts of James, giving them an ethereal quality that spoke of the madness of Ophelia more than the purity and piousness of Desdemona. Initially, Garrick organised searches on her behalf, an attempt to quell her sense of abandonment and loss. Her grief.

The duke had reappeared for an evening performance at the theatre, a dark look on his face at all times. He kept his distance from Charlotte, his black eyes glittering with a quiet fury whenever she appeared on stage.

Garrick couldn't help but fear that Frederick had come for James and may come for him as well as the architect of his heartache. He began to harbour a resentment towards Charlotte for throwing away everything he had built for them. For ruining them both.

Finally, the duke appeared at Garrick's suite.

"Did you know that she would betray me?" Frederick glowered.

"I knew that she did not reciprocate your affections the way you wished. As did you, I think."

"I did. But if I cannot have her, no man shall."

Garrick felt a stab of guilt and sorrow in his gut. It had gone further than he had intended, and they were all caught in an inescapable trap.

"What did you do to him? Her husband?" he asked in a quiet voice.

"Nothing that the life under the waves of the river will not be finding to their liking."

Garrick felt a pang of guilt. James was an innocent in this, and his death was partially on Garrick's hands.

"And what of the rest of us?"

"Be damned for all I care. I am finished with this theatre, and with you. My brother and I shall no longer be your patrons after this insult. I cannot watch her on the stage knowing that she betrayed me thus. She is mine, damned or no." The duke's voice raised, filled with anger and bile, until he could no longer maintain it, and he coughed into a modestly monogrammed handkerchief.

"But, my lord—"

The duke raised his hand to silence Garrick. The handkerchief fell to the floor, unnoticed.

"We are finished, Garrick. It is done. There is no stopping what is to come."

He strode from the suite and out of the theatre.

Garrick watched him disappear down the corridor, an anger surging in him.

This is all her fault.

She hadn't listened, hadn't done what she was told. He would make amends with the duke; he had to. If his choice was to save Charlotte or the theatre, he knew which would win out.

He stared at the square of white linen on the floor.

He knew what the duke demanded of him, even if he left it unsaid.

***

In her dressing room, Charlotte quietly wept. April had arrived, bringing with it cool winds and showers. James was still missing after two weeks of searching, and she feared the worst.

Worse still, the performances still had to go on, the crowds bayed for her, and she had no choice but to wander through performance after performance in a daze, her mind fixed on James. In the final weeks of the season, her performance would no longer be of note, or so she believed.

The second performance of April ran smoothly despite her conflicting thoughts. Flowers and praise were lavished upon her just as richly as ever, and she felt a moment of joy in an otherwise bleak existence.

Looking at the royal box, she could make out the figure of the duke, his glowering eyes fixed on her as he stood to leave. It was his final visit, she understood; this was to be his final goodbye to the theatre, and to her.

Returning to her room after the performance, Charlotte sat in a daze, staring at her own reflection. She mourned for James, for the life they could have had. She felt the blame of his disappearance hanging around her neck like a rope.

In the mirror's surface, she thought she saw movement, a flicker over her shoulder. Turning around, the room was empty.

Facing back to the mirror, she was greeted by the reflection of James, his face greyed and green with rot, his eyes missing, hollow voids of blood and gore. His jaw was only bone, the skin bitten away, tendons snapped and muscle peeled. A large gash in the side of his head poured blood, which floated upwards as if caught in a current. His clothing was ragged and torn, revealing a grey and bloated body, dark veins of rot crossing over pallid flesh. The smell of damp and decay overwhelmed her.

A bony, decaying hand reached out towards her in the mirror.

"Charlotte—"

She screamed, scrambling backwards, away from the vision of her dead love. The glass exploded, cutting her arms and fingers as she instinctively covered her face with them.

"Charlotte—"

She ran for the door, desperate to escape. It wouldn't open. She pulled with all her might, but it was no use.

The door was locked from the outside.

Glancing back, the room was empty, the shattered mirror simply glass. Looking at her hands, the cuts were gone.

She pounded on the door.

"Help me, I'm locked in! Hello? Can anyone hear me? I need aid! Help me!"

Outside the locked door, a shadow moved.

There was a click as the key turned in the lock and the door opened. A dark figure stood in the doorway.

Charlotte stared for a moment, her heart pounding as relief flooded through her.

"Garrick, oh thank the Lord above! I was terrified! Someone locked me in, and I saw the most awful vision!"

He walked into the room as she spoke. She turned to face him as the tears fell down her cheeks.

"Sshhh." He placed his arms around her, holding her in a fatherly embrace. "It's all alright now, I'm here."

"But who would lock me in?!" she sobbed as she buried her face in his shoulder.

"Maybe someone blames you for the wrath of the Duke of York and wanted to hold you to ransom."

"What?" She looked up, and in a shard of mirror that remained in the frame, she saw the glint of a dagger being raised behind his back.

She gasped.

"Garrick? No!"

"It is the will of the duke. I will have amends, even if I must spill your blood to do it."

With a cry, Charlotte ran, ran towards the darkness of the stage.

Chapter 12

London, 2025

Hazel's eyes opened slowly, squinting slightly as she groggily took in her surroundings. The smell of cleaning materials and bodily fluids hung in the air, crisp white light peeking through her eyelids as they opened. A dull roar of chatter and beeps settled around her.

A calm, dulcet voice that was so familiar to her suddenly sounded, close to her. It sounded like home.

"Hazel, are you alright? Still with us?"

Marianne gently rubbed her cheek as Hazel's eyes opened the rest of the way, and she groaned. Shc felt heavy, like her limbs had been weighted down with sleep.

She was in a hospital ward, her arm hooked up to a drip of clear liquid slowly dispensing into an injection port on her arm.

A nurse bustled over to her bed.

"Now then, finally awake, are we?"

"What happened?"

"You took a bit of a knock, but you're alright. Just lie back, someone will be with you shortly."

"What's this for?" Hazel gestured at her arm.

"Oh, that? Just saline, we had to keep you hydrated."

The nurse moved to the next bed, the conversation over.

"What happened?" Hazel asked Marianne.

"You and Tom were found in the basement. You were unconscious, and Tom—well, Tom was hurt really badly. Warner called an ambulance for you both."

The basement. It all came back to her—Charlotte. The dream suddenly flowed back into her memory.

Garrick. The whole time it was Garrick.

"I need to get out of here. I have to go back. I need to finish what I started, Marianne. I need to finish the play."

"The play can wait; you already finished it. There's no way Warner will let you back down there now, not after that. Hazel, Tom is dead, for Christ's sake. He died in the ambulance on the way here."

Hazel gasped, a sudden vision of Tom lying on the ground, still, a pool of blood slowly spreading from the side of his head, clouding her mind.

"Tom, no!" she cried, heavy tears welling in her eyes. Another death in the theatre. Another death that was her fault. Marianne held her hand, looking at her with pity.

"It wasn't your fault, Hazel. He fell, right? It was an accident."

"No, it wasn't. It was the same evil spirit that killed Daniel. And I'm going to get it if it is the last thing I do."

***

As soon as she was released from the hospital and the theatre was open to staff again following Tom's death in the basement, Hazel made her way there. It was no surprise the basement door was locked once again. After all, it was dangerous.

The dream she had experienced played out in her head over and over again: the death of James, Frederick's anger, and Garrick's role in Charlotte's death. She needed to change the play.

Calling for a meeting with Warner, the director, and the cast, she outlined the changes to the script. The cast and director were horrified to find changes so close to opening night, and negotiations soon began, Hazel re-writing the script even as the meeting continued around her. Eventually, a final play was settled upon and new lines distributed.

Halliwell was no longer to be positioned on the false walkway but would still appear in the final scene. The walkway would instead be occupied by Gregory Issacs, who jumped at the chance to turn his portrayal of Garrick into something darker. *This could be my big break*, he thought as he stared at Halliwell from the corner of his eye, a smug smile slowly drawing the corners of his mouth upwards.

The death and disappearance of James would be added to dialogue but not shown on stage; Warner insisted on that.

Rehearsals would soon be underway, a mad scramble to make the new ending work and make up for lost time. Rumours had spread of the cursed production at the Theatre Royal, and the first week of performances was sold out. People whispered of the play that had so many accidents and deaths associated with it. They whispered of ghostly curses and murderous conspiracies.

Hazel watched the rehearsals unfold each day, all the while waiting for the dark entity to strike. She could feel it lurking, watching her, a constant companion. But the scent of rose and honey also drifted across the auditorium, reminding her that Charlotte would be free if she had the courage to carry on.

It was the morning of the final dress rehearsal when her final purchase from the wiccan websites she had perused arrived, and her kit for trapping a spirit was finally complete—Paolo Santo incense and a bundle of sage for burning. The holy water she had taken from St. Pauls, her antique candlesticks, and a large supply of salt completed her kit for trapping the shadow. For banishment, she added five black candles, and a bag of crystals—amethyst and obsidian—for banishment and protection. She hoped the wiccan message boards had been right, but there was no turning back. To this kit, she added chalk, a torch, and a crowbar.

As the dress rehearsal began under the watchful eye of Warner, Hazel slipped away with her bag of supplies. Grabbing a screwdriver from an abandoned toolkit in the maintenance room, she made her way to the locked basement door.

At the door, she dropped the bag, studying the lock. She had seen a lot of movies where a credit card or a simple hair-pin could open a locked door, but she knew real life didn't work like that. Using the screwdriver, she moved to the side of the door away from the lock and unscrewed the four screws on each hinge plate. Using the crowbar for leverage, she pulled the hinges free of the wall. With a painful grunt, the door slowly pulled forwards, snapping the lock mechanism and falling forwards. With all the strength she could muster, she caught it and lowered the door to the ground, cushioning any noise from the falling door.

Picking up her bag, she stepped into the corridor and went down the stairs into the basement. The air smelled metallic, Tom's blood lingering in the poorly ventilated space. A dark patch stained the ground where he had fallen, the theatre chair still lying there. Stepping around the marked floor, crossing to the metal cabinet, she opened it to find a shovel and broom, just as Tom had said. She set to work drawing an outline in chalk over the ground—a large circle, the centre containing a double-sided arrow crossed with a staff. Smaller circles and lines on each side of the central cross completed the design.

To this, she added salt and holy water, carefully leaving the side nearest the broken wall untouched. Finally, the circular design with wiccan symbols was covered with loose dirt from the floor, obscuring it from view, a silver candlestick placed at the top and bottom of the design for purity.

Her work complete, she headed for the hole in the wall. It was time to see what secrets lay under that patch of floor. As she raised her leg to enter the secret room, she felt a rush of cold air behind her, a darkness blossoming over the room. She stopped.

It was there.

Stepping back into the main room, she stood firm as the spirit wrapped around her, a cloak of evil and darkness.

Fighting through the weight of the spirit that held her, Hazel fell to her knees. From her pocket, she pulled out the remains of the holy water and salt and scattered them beside her.

The circle was complete. There was a glimmer in the air, a light in the darkness, and the shadow lifted from her. She jumped back, careful to avoid scuffing the line of salt and blessed water, and looked at the shadow.

Pushing against an invisible boundary, the darkness screamed. Various shades of blackness railed and pulsed against the forces that held it.

The spirit was trapped. This was her chance to find Charlotte.

As quickly as her legs would allow, she climbed into the secret room, reaching back through the hole to grab the broom, shovel, and her bag of remaining supplies. As an added layer of precaution, she drew another salt line at the base of the wall. Nothing would stop her this time.

At the far side of the room, she saw the patch of ground that was darker than the rest. Using the broom to sweep away the loose dirt and dust that obscured her view, she found a group of floorboards of a much darker colour. Using the crowbar for leverage, Hazel lifted the time-softened, decaying boards one at a time. When the second board lifted, she saw it.

A wisp of white hair, caught on a nail.

A skull.

Her skeleton, small and fragile, had been dumped here beneath the floor. Charlotte was there, her body left to rot and decay under the theatre that she loved, forgotten. Her skeleton had survived fire and centuries of performances, resting there all the while.

Hazel wept with relief.

"I found you. I found you."

"You found me," a soft, lyrical voice came from behind her. Charlotte was standing in the basement beyond the salted hole in the wall. She smiled at Hazel, a benevolent smile that gave out a warmth Hazel felt in her heart.

"What now, Charlotte? Will you be freed?"

"Tell my story. Free me from my captor. Then I shall know freedom and peace again."

Charlotte disappeared.

The darkness screamed.

Winding a crystal of amethyst and one of obsidian around her neck, Hazel moved back into the main basement. Moving around the outskirts of the room, she lit five black candles and placed them on the ground at equal distances from each other. Finally, she lit the herbs and incense, allowing the smoke to slowly fill the room. It roiled and spilled over the black mass trapped in the circle, creating a dense, dark fog.

"I know you, Garrick. Reveal yourself."

The spirit growled. The shape shifted, pulling against itself. Shrinking and changing, Hazel could make out features emerging. The statue from the foyer. Garrick was there.

"You are not welcome in this place, Garrick. You will leave it."

"This theatre is mine!" A roaring voice filled the room. The face in the shifting black smoke screamed, echoing and reverberating until Hazel feared her head might burst.

"No more! This theatre has not been yours for two hundred years. And it never will be yours again!" Hazel's voice raised to a shout.

"She must remain here. She is mine to keep."

"She will be free. And you will leave this place!"

"No!"

Hazel threw crystals in a scattered pattern across the floor.

"I banish you, David Garrick! Leave!" Hazel screamed until her voice gave out.

The black shape twisted, growing smaller as Garrick's scream grew louder, matching her own. There was a flash of light, a column of fire that rose within the circle, growing brighter and hotter as it met the darkness of Garrick's form. With a final cry, the darkness disappeared and the flame retreated. The fire extinguished. Light returned to the basement.

She had done it.

Garrick was gone.

Chapter 13

The first performance began without incident, every cue was hit, every line spoken to perfection, despite it being such a new version of the script. The dress rehearsal had been disjointed, but they had muddled through their new lines somehow. Now, with a captive audience before them, they were perfection. Each actor in the company was undertaking their finest role with this production; they could feel it.

Charlotte's tale unfolded as they danced over the stage—talented star of the stage turned into a prisoner of the society that made her. Intrigue and murder, it was clear the audience was being led on a journey that spoke to their souls before they would be left broken and shocked by the explosive ending.

Hazel watched from the back of the auditorium, finally able to let herself enjoy the moment that her work was being performed for a sold-out audience and Charlotte's story was being told.

Warner had the skeletal remains removed under cover of night and taken to University College London, where the Forensic Anthropology department would research further before she could be given a proper, named burial. While he knew he couldn't stop the news from breaking, he could at least control when it did.

The secret room had been sealed with plastic sheeting, ready for the university to bring in archaeologists to study the items. Hazel had a feeling the bloody handkerchief would cause a lot of rumour and mystery.

The candles, chalk, and crystals Hazel managed to remove before they were seen by anyone else, but the strange smell in the air lingered in Warner's nostrils when she took him to the basement. His suspicions over the broken door and smoke were very obvious.

Hazel had been let go from her contract of a second play, her task complete. Warner was not willing to risk another play that led to catastrophe and mayhem, and Hazel couldn't blame him for that, however upset she was at losing her perfect role. Tonight's play would be the only performance she would ever see, but that would be enough if she could see Charlotte freed.

The play wound on towards its close. Marianne's portrayal of Charlotte was as close to reality as Hazel could have hoped, and the scene of her finding James missing broke Hazel's heart.

It was towards the end of the play that Hazel noticed a glimmer of red and white in the wing of the stage. Charlotte, in her red dress and bejewelled pendant, was watching Marianne intently on the stage, a strange look on her face. It was a calculated look, her lips set in a sneer that gave her face a cruel look Hazel had not seen before. Sneaking out of the auditorium, Hazel headed towards the backstage area as Marianne exited the stage.

Hazel reached the backstage corridor just in time to see Marianne burst through the door from the stage wing, bent double, clutching her stomach. Choking coughs escaped her throat as she stumbled, gasping for breath, her face twisted in pain.

"Marianne!" Hazel cried, rushing forwards. Grabbing Marianne by the shoulders, staring at her face with concern, Hazel started. As she looked, Marianne's green eyes flashed an icy grey, draining of colour.

"Marianne! Are you alright?"

With long gasps, Marianne's breathing began to calm, the coughing subsiding. She stood up a little straighter and shook Hazel off.

"I'm fine, thank you. I don't know what came over me."

Her voice sounded strange. It had a clipped tone, with each syllable enunciated as if she was learning to speak. Or speaking with a borrowed voice.

"Marianne, look at me."

Those eyes. Green and grey all at the same time. Familiar but cold.

"I have to go. I must get to the stage. They need me."

"Charlotte?" Hazel asked cautiously, her face pale. "Is that you?"

Marianne smiled slowly, a half-smile Hazel had seen before—on Charlotte's face.

Hazel felt her body freeze, weighted to the floor.

"It is working. I grow stronger every moment. But I must help them tell my story."

"Give Marianne back. This isn't right! Let her go!"

"After the performance, I promise. I will be free, as will she. I give you my word."

"This isn't right, Charlotte. Not like this."

"It will be over soon, I promise. Thank you for all you have done for me." With that, Charlotte, in Marianne's body, turned, her dress floating behind her, and glided back through the door to the stage and out of sight.

After a moment, Hazel felt the life returning to her limbs and, still reeling from the shock, followed after Marianne.

***

On stage, Garrick and the Duke of York concluded their heated conversation, and Halliwell strode off, his white handkerchief left on the stage. Garrick picked it up, and placed it in his pocket before turning to the audience, where Isaacs delivered a haunting monologue.

"Lost. All lost. Everything I have worked for, yearned for, gone in the blink of an eye. And why? Love? No, obsession. All she had to do was pretend, and this would have been ended. Were we not all prisoners in this tale?

"The duke, beholden to a loveless marriage. And I? Beholden to my duty, my love of this place. More alive than any person, the blood of a thousand performances running in her veins, the voices of thousands still to come filling her halls. She is mine and I am hers. She must endure.

"And now? That pious harlot throws it away and damns us all. This is her fault. Her husband? Gone. He floats under the waters ebb, forgotten and alone. Her future? Gone. Her life? Uncertain. I cannot let the theatre fall for her whims. No. It shall not be. I shall have my place in history; all shall be forgiven. And the theatre shall watch all and endure."

With thunderous applause echoing in his mind, Isaacs left the stage. He bumped into Marianne in the wing, with Hazel not far behind.

"Marianne, they love us! Are you ready for the finale?" he hissed. She smiled and nodded, leaning in closely to him.

"I'm ready. The world will know the truth soon enough. Let's have a kiss for luck."

Before he could reply, she kissed him, a slow kiss that pinned him in place. He felt strange, as if something was hunting him, slowly seeking him out. Then he felt it—a tickle, like a wisp of smoke, dancing on his tongue and pouring down his throat.

His eyes, a dull brown, flashed grey as Charlotte's spirit took root in him, her memory taking over his mind, all scripts forgotten. Her mark on him complete, the seed planted, she retreated. She stepped away, breaking the kiss.

Hazel watched, dumbfounded.

Isaacs stumbled backwards, shaken.

"Ready, Mister Garrick?" Charlotte said in a silky voice that was both sweet and hopeful, with a note of danger. He didn't know why, but Isaacs felt as if he was an animal lost in a strange land. And somewhere out of sight lurked a predator he couldn't see.

Charlotte stepped onto the stage and sat at the table in the dressing room set, blinking in the glare from the stage light.

So much less elegant than candlelight and lanterns, she thought. The audience gazed up at her, glittering eyes in the dark, full of admiration. For the first time in over two hundred years, Charlotte felt alive. She was home.

A hushed whisper. A cough. A rustling sound. All that life, waiting for her, finally seeing her as she softly wept on the stage. Taking a deep breath, she relived the vision of James's ghost, a horrific image displayed of a rotted, bloated corpse that lingered before her. In her centuries of loneliness and isolation as she wandered the theatre, that image had played on her memory more than anything.

As she pictured the image of James in her mind, a harrowing vision appeared on the stage before her—grey, with peeling skin and maggots crawling over empty eye sockets. Not as terrifying as the skinless being she had seen all those centuries ago, but a new horror that squirmed and bit under her skin. She let out a piercing scream and scrambled back.

The audience shrieked, screaming in unison.

"She didn't scream like that in rehearsals. I almost believed that," whispered the stage manager to Halliwell backstage as Charlotte wrestled with the locked dressing room door.

"Always save the best for them, dear boy," Halliwell replied, gesturing to the audience. "It's the actor's way."

Isaacs stepped onto the stage, his hand carefully hidden behind his back.

"Garrick, oh, thank the Lord above! I was terrified! Someone locked me in, and I saw the most awful vision!"

"Sshhh. It's all alright now, I'm here."

"But who would lock me in?!"

"Maybe someone blames you for the wrath of the Duke of York and wanted to hold you to ransom."

"What?"

The dagger was raised.

"Garrick? No!"

She ran off stage. The lights went down.

The director, sitting inside the tech booth, looked up in shock.

"They've gone off book!"

Halliwell, in the deep recesses of the stage wing, marched up to Hazel.

"Have you made changes again? I can't work like this, you know. Amateur!" He didn't wait for a reply, storming off, ready to salvage the final scene.

"I haven't!" she cried after him.

On the stage again, the lights came back to reveal Charlotte and Garrick, a mask on his face to create the shadow effect. The harness used by Marianne secured Charlotte to the drop.

Charlotte ran across the false walkway, with Garrick right behind her. Pulling at her dress, he pulled her backwards into a tight embrace.

"Please don't do this, I've done nothing! Help me, please!"

The rope wrapped tightly around her throat.

"Spare your lies, you painted whore. Rot and perish, and be damned."

The necklace was ripped from her, falling to the stage.

"Stop—"

She fell. Jolting to the ground, the stage drop engaged, pulling Charlotte short. Too quickly. Charlotte was not as practiced as Marianne; the timing was off. Blood dripped from her face. She could feel Marianne buried inside her, nursing her bruised ribs, afraid and alone.

"Goodbye, Desdemona. May you never know peace for your betrayal," Garrick uttered, walking to the end of the walkway and out of sight, his mask now free.

He reappeared on the stage, staring up at Charlotte's hanging body. He slowly bent down and picked up the golden pendant that lay on the stage.

The room was utterly silent.

"I think you might want this back, your Grace," he said to the empty stage. Halliwell stepped on stage. Confusion lined his face as he scrambled to improvise. This was not the cue he expected.

"What is this?" He took the pendant and stared at it for a moment before looking up, trying to get the play back on track. "What have you done, Garrick?"

"Just as you wanted, your Grace."

"I did not want this. We must cut her down! She may yet be saved!" Halliwell ran off stage and onto the walkway, miming cutting the rope from above with his costume sword. With a strain in his voice, he lowered Charlotte to the ground as gently as he could.

Issacs calmly walked to her, drawing his dagger. With one swift, smooth motion, he cut her throat. The audience gasped.

"Garrick, no!" Halliwell cried from the walkway above, once again disappearing off stage with a slight scowl that the audience couldn't see.

As Halliwell reappeared on the stage, Garrick brought forth a white square of linen, smoothly wiping the blade on the fabric—the handkerchief discarded by the duke.

"You have been careless with your possessions, your Grace."

"Charlotte," Halliwell wept, cradling her body.

"Come man, you wanted her out of your life after her lies. You murdered her husband. Don't play the grieving lover now. It doesn't become you."

"What madness has befallen you?"

"The theatre must endure. We will hide her, together. You will continue in your patronage or I shall expose your deed to the world. Who will the world believe cruelly dispatched Charlotte? Her benevolent benefactor," he gestured to himself, "or her jilted and powerful lover?" he gestured at Halliwell.

"So be it. But I will not let this die, Garrick. I will have your blood for this."

"Then my blood shall be spilled for a worthy cause. This theatre was built on blood, and on blood it will remain. If I shall die, my soul shall live on in this place, an eternal guard."

"I shall see you and your theatre fall for this, Garrick."

"You can try, but you know it would serve you no good. I have helped you, and you owe me. Now, it is your turn to help me. We bury her here, in the depths of the theatre. She can remain here, in the place she loved, forever. Would you not want that for her?"

Warner clenched his teeth in anger, looking for Hazel.

Halliwell nodded, tears running down his cheeks. His improvisational skills were rusty, but his chest swelled with pride for his performance tonight.

"And our secrets shall go to the grave with us. Do we have an accord?" Isaacs continued.

Halliwell nodded, his head held high.

"We have an accord. Never a word of this shall be spoken. I shall go to Prussia, your theatre be damned. I cannot bear the knowledge of this."

Lifting Charlotte, the two men walked off stage.

A moment later, Charlotte reappeared, alone on the stage, blood staining her pale face.

"And so here shall my soul remain, in the theatre I loved so. Betrayed by those I trusted, doomed to walk these halls forevermore.

"The years came and went. I saw it all. The whole of time contained in this place. I felt the flames as they licked at the stage, cold to the touch but sparkling. Around me, the world fell and was rebuilt, new and shiny but somehow old and wise.

"I saw it all in my loneliness. Always here, never seen. Reliving my final moments as the world turned without me. But maybe, tonight, in this dark space, maybe I have finally been given peace."

The stage lights went down.

The house lights came up, thunderous applause reaching the rafters.

Taking her bow, Charlotte looked over the adoring crowd, a single tear running down her cheek. It was done. Her story had been told.

***

Hazel waited in a corridor backstage as Charlotte exited. Her work had been done, and now Charlotte could be free.

"Charlotte!" she called, seeing her gracefully walk towards her. "Is it done? Is it over?"

"It is over." Charlotte smiled, a gracious and warm smile that wrapped around Hazel, squeezing her tightly. "Thanks to you, Garrick is gone and my soul is free. That tiresome man held me for too long." Her smile turned cold, a cruel glint in grey eyes that should have been sea green.

"What do you mean?"

"Do you have any idea what it is like, watching other less-talented people taking the spotlight that was ripped away from you? How a place you loved becomes a prison? For two and a half centuries, I have watched, unseen, unknown, and unloved, waiting for my moment to destroy this place again. I almost succeeded once. Garrick tried to stop me; for so long, he held me at bay, desperate to save his precious theatre and everyone in it," she spat.

"No, you can't have. Not you!"

"I thought if this place could burn it would end. But he saw me; he tried to stop me. He died trying. Always a martyr. For centuries, he held me captive, weak, guarding my body to keep me from growing in power, saving this place from destruction. But then, you all found Garrick's secret room, and suddenly, I was seen again, my face on the wall. Now, thanks to you there's no one left to stop me. And I am finally free. The world shall burn, starting with the theatre that betrayed me. All thanks to you."

"You're twisted. I trusted you! You made me believe you were good!"

"I was. I am. And then I died alone, screaming into the dark and the cold. Betrayed. No one would help me. My adoring public, they just turned their backs and watched me suffer and fall. Then everyone forgot me. When you stare into the darkness alone for so long, eventually something stares back. It is time for the world to pay for what was done to me."

"Bring Marianne back, now. You gave your word!"

"The word of an actress." She smiled, looking at Hazel in mock sympathy. "So sweet, so simple. So trusting. No, I believe I'll keep her. I like the way her skin feels. But don't worry, she's still in here, tucked away safe and sound."

"Bring her back! What Garrick did to you was unforgiveable, but he's gone now. You can't blame the world for what happened! And you can't have Marianne."

"I can, and I will. The world is owed nothing. Full of sycophants, liars, and pain. You think the world has moved on? Nothing has changed. We are still bought and sold with sweet words and empty promises. The same cruelty, hiding behind a mask of progress."

A low rumble began beside Hazel's feet, and she thought she saw her shadow lengthen and move before her. She felt the world shake, unnoticed by anyone but her.

The air behind Charlotte glimmered and shifted, faces appearing and disappearing in a fine mist. Hazel briefly smiled a small smile as she looked at Charlotte, the only witness to the movement in the air.

"Your soul is broken, isn't it? I'll stop you, Charlotte."

"No, Hazel. I don't believe you will. You've forgotten your bag of tricks this time."

"I don't need a bag of tricks. You were so focused on destruction and your own freedom, you forgot one thing."

"What is that?"

"You aren't the only person to die in this place. And some of them aren't happy with you."

The air filled with smoke. Daniel, Tom, and a host of spirits appeared in the murky gloom, surrounding Charlotte. Victims from the fire that destroyed the theatre. The fire that Charlotte was to blame for. All victims of Charlotte in one way or another, and here to lay claim to her soul.

Working as one, ethereal arms reached for Marianne, pulling her body taut. Reaching inside her, they began to pull. As they did, the soul of Charlotte began to emerge, screaming, from Marianne's body.

"Hazel, we have her. When she leaves Marianne, grab her and run!" Daniel's disembodied voice whispered in Hazel's ear.

With a guttural cry, Charlotte was ripped from Marianne. Grabbing an arm, Hazel pulled Marianne free from the circle of spirits. Fire consumed them, spreading to Charlotte's soul, which ignited fully. Her screams filled Hazel's veins, feeling her cry in each pulse of her heart. Her once pale skin blackened, her hair burned to nothing, her icy eyes melted in the fury of the fiery spirits.

Finally, Charlotte grew quiet. Her soul was reduced to ash.

With a small smile and a nod of thanks, Daniel and Tom looked at Hazel.

"I'm sorry," she said to them both, tears streaking her face.

"It is forgiven. Tell our families we love them, that we are alright. Please?"

"I will, I promise."

The spirits disappeared into the ether.

Hazel pulled Marianne through the corridors of the theatre to the stage door and into the street.

"Come on, Marianne, we need to get out of here."

"Hazel? What happened?" Marianne asked quietly, weak and confused. Hazel kissed her on the forehead.

"Don't worry, you're alright. I'll explain everything when we get home."

No one noticed the glowing ember that remained of Charlotte's soul, burning steadily and slowly.

Epilogue

Marianne spotted Hazel across the room and gave her a bright smile. They embraced, sharing a quick kiss.

"No touching!" a stern voice cut across the room.

"Sorry," Hazel said, nodding at the prison guard as they sat at the small table. She smoothed her standard-issue grey jumper as she looked at Marianne, staring into her eyes, as sea-green and lovely as they had ever been, her red hair fiery and wild. She looked radiant.

"You look good. How are you?"

"I'm fine," Marianne replied. "I'm at the Apollo Theatre now, rehearsing for *Punch* later this year. Serious drama, I might be in with a shot of an Olivier award. And you? How are you holding up?"

"Oh, you know." Hazel gestured vaguely.

"They're going to rebuild the theatre, did you hear?"

"Warner must be overjoyed," Hazel said flatly.

"Don't be like that. I haven't spoken to him. Not since he—well, since he had you arrested for setting that fire."

"Made for a nice headline for him, I'll bet. *Disgruntled Employee Turns Arsonist.*" She waved a hand in the air as if displaying a billboard.

"I don't think it was like that," Marianne started.

"Well, what was it like then? Face it, I'm the scapegoat. You know I didn't set that fire."

"Well, you did get us out of there very quickly, and you were acting strangely. People died, Hazel."

"I was trying to help you. Do you still not remember anything?"

"I remember you shouting, and a lot of applause, but nothing else. Just the fire on the news, and Halliwell. I'm sorry I couldn't be your alibi, but I just don't remember."

"No one is sorrier for Halliwell's death than I am. I didn't set the fire. It was Charlotte, I swear it. Do you really think I'm capable of this?"

"The ghost again, Hazel? This is why the police didn't believe you."

"And you?" Hazel looked intently into Marianne's eyes, hoping for a flicker of sympathy, some sign that she believed her.

Her green eyes were grey.

"Marianne?"

Marianne smiled slowly.

"Charlotte?"

"There is one thing the dead spiritualist should have taught you. Always make sure every bit of the spirit is gone when you try to destroy them. Otherwise, it's just so easy for us to come crawling back."

"Marianne, please, come back to me!" Hazel grabbed her by the hands. Suddenly, she was pulled back in her chair.

"I said no touching!" The guard's grip on her was strong.

Marianne stood, Charlotte's cold eyes staring out at Hazel.

"Well, I think that concludes our meeting, then. Lovely to see you, Hazel. I'm sorry that your friends can't help you now."

"Charlotte, stop! Don't do this. Remember who you were—the kind, sweet woman that was adored by everyone who knew her."

"She is dead and gone. Goodbye, darling. I have a life to enjoy and an adoring crowd to greet. Before it's too late for them, anyway. Thank you for everything."

Hazel watched in horror as Charlotte walked to the secure door. With a buzz, the door slid open, and she was gone.

The guard released Hazel, and she jumped to her feet, rushing to the door.

It was locked.

Charlotte was free.

About the Author

Known for her gothic prose, dark poetry, and historical flair, Catriona exploded onto the indie horror scene in 2025 with her debut collection of short stories and poetry, *Beyond The Smoke And Shadow,* and some anthology contributions. She lives in Swindon, Wiltshire, with her author partner, Jim Ody, his three wonderful children, and their extensive skull collection. She is currently working on new projects for 2026.

Facebook: @Catriona Mowat Author
Instagram & Threads: @Catriona.mowat.author
TikTok: @Catrionamowat.author
Bluesky: @catmowat.bsky.social

Acknowledgements

Thank you to you for reading my gothic novella. Every reader makes writing worthwhile, and I am so glad you took the time to read my work with so many incredible titles to choose from in the world.

Thank you to Heather Larson from Indie Terror 13 Editing, you keep me sane and spot the errors that are in my blind spot. Thank you so much for being a voice of reason!

Thank you to Christy from Grim Poppy Design for the cover image, once again you had the perfect image for me, and I love it!

To my Beta and ARC readers: you are amazing, thank you so much for everything you do.

To Jim, Siobhan, Dad, Muriel, and my family and friends, thank you for all of your support, advice, and encouragement. It means more than you know.

I count myself so blessed so have so many amazing friends in the community, and particularly from the *Indie Horror Chapter* and online communities. You keep me going. In particular, a massive thanks to Daniel J. Barnes, Amy Rollinson, Jen Ramsden,

Rhiannon Williams, Sharron Joy Reads, Emma Oulton, Chris Jones, Chiara Cooper, Alexus Johnson, Stephen Barnard, Candace Nola, E.C. Samuels, Gemma Wilkinson, Tom Carter, Guy Quintero, Kealan Patrick Burke, Matthew Cash, Matthew Clarke, Kev Harrison, Alyssa Cook, Lisa Breanne, Simon Bleaken, Kayla Frederick, Kimberley Nicole, Jyl Glenn, Matthew Lutton, Ashley Lister, Graeme Reynolds, Trish Wilson, Rachel Gregory, Susana Aires, Mason Marks, Chris Harrison, Milt Theodossiou, Stephanie Huddle, Alexandra Nisneru, and Brad Thomas.

I am so grateful to you all.

Content Warnings

- Emotional abuse in a relationship, including coercion and financial control.
- Chauvinism, including GBV
- Mental health, auditory/visual hallucinations
- Implication of suicide.
- Minimal gore.
- Scenes of death and violence/murder, including hanging, strangulation, and cut throat.
- Imprisonment.
- Bereavement including loss of parents and spouse.
- Minimal inclusion of confined spaces, and locations at height.
- Hospitalisation (brief)
- Relation breakdown including divorce (briefly mentioned, not described in detail)

www.ingramcontent.com/pod-product-compliance
Ingram Content Group UK Ltd.
Pitfield, Milton Keynes, MK11 3LW, UK
UKHW041853290725
461340UK00004B/111

9 781068 217913